SPLIT SCREAM

VOLUME SIX

Featuring:

DAVID CORSE

&

RYAN T. JENKINS

SPLIT SCREAM, Volume Six © 2024 by David Corse, Ryan T. Jenkins, Alex Ebenstein, and Tenebrous Press

All rights reserved. No parts of this publication may be reproduced, distributed or transmitted in any form by any means, except for brief excerpts for the purpose of review, without the prior written consent of the owner. All inquiries should be addressed to tenebrouspress@gmail.com.

Published by Tenebrous Press.
Visit our website at www.tenebrouspress.com.

First Printing, November 2024.

The characters and events portrayed in this work are fictitious. Any similarity to real persons, living or dead (except for satirical purposes), is coincidental and not intended by the author.

Print ISBN: 978-1-959790-25-9
eBook ISBN: 978-1-959790-26-6

Cover illustrations by Evangeline Gallagher.

Interior illustrations by Echo Echo.

Cover and interior design by Dreadful Designs.

Edited by Alex Ebenstein.

Production of this book was made possible in part by a grant from the Regional Arts & Culture Council. Visit https://racc.org/ for more information.

For the ones who like it weird.

INTRODUCTION

The novelette has been dismissed and disparaged. Some dictionaries don't even define them as a unique form, listing only short stories, novellas, or novels. Others write them off as being "too sentimental" or "trivial".

This is silly, of course, and, with little effort it's easy to see the novelette has a purpose and value.

What makes a novelette, then? Exact word counts vary, but these stories are longer than a short story and shorter than a novella. In this case, between ten and twenty thousand words; or, horror you can devour in about an hour or two.

Sound like another form of storytelling?

I'm not saying a novelette is a movie is a novelette. And I'm not saying written fiction *needs* to be like movies. But… But they are *kind of* like movies in terms of length and threads, right? If you're willing to accept that premise, at least for the moment, may I present to you…

SPLIT SCREAM
A Novelette Double Feature

Truly, what better way to present these stories than as a double feature? Do you *have* to read them back to back in a single Friday night after dusk? Certainly not. But could you? Absolutely.

Shall we?

This volume features a couple tales of messed up familial relationships. First is David Corse's "Mother is Coming Home," a toxic mother-son relationship dealing with the discovery of a flesh-like portal on their property. Ryan T. Jenkins's "Come to Daddy" follows, where a strung-out, deluded man reckons with getting divorced from his wife and son while navigating his new home haunted by a movie poster of a certain B-list actor.

What do you think? You ready? Grab some popcorn, turn the lights low, and don't be afraid to scream.

This is Volume Six of SPLIT SCREAM, the series firmly rolling along now through Tenebrous Press. It's all good from here, eh?

Whether this is your first time with us, or you've read one of the previous five volumes—thanks for stopping by.

Long live the novelette!

Alex Ebenstein
Tenebrous Press
Michigan, USA
August 2024

CONTENTS

MOTHER IS COMING HOME 5
David Corse

COME TO DADDY 93
Ryan T. Jenkins

ABOUT THE AUTHORS 178

ACKNOWLEDGMENTS 179

ABOUT THE ARTISTS 183

CONTENT WARNINGS 184

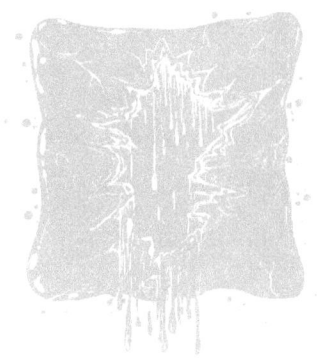

MOTHER IS COMING HOME
David Corse

The clang of Mother's handbell shatters Otis's euphoria. He's at the foot of his bed, admiring a pair of pressed khakis he plans to wear during his trip to New York City. Annoyed, he gently places the pants inside his leather suitcase and reminds himself that he'll be away from Mother for an entire week.

"Do you hear me?" Mother shouts before ringing her bell again, louder this time. It's like a bomb going off in his ears. Every day, all day long, she summons him with her brass bell and orders him about. He wishes Amelia—

Mother's best friend—never gave her the infernal torture device.

"Coming," he yells back and heads to the top of the stairs. Halfway there, he stops to make himself presentable. He re-tucks his white short-sleeved, button-down shirt into his jeans and adjusts his glasses so they rest perfectly on the bridge of his nose. Mother likes when he looks nice.

"What is it, Mother?" he says, stepping to the landing.

Below, Rebecca Ferryman glares at him from her wheelchair. Her gray hair and makeup are immaculate, and her white and green floral dress is spotless. Without a word, she rings her handbell violently, reminding him that when she calls, he needs to come. Ten seconds pass, then twenty, then thirty.

Otis's jaw clenches, and he squeezes his eyes shut in frustration. To soothe himself, he imagines his future: Times Square, Madison Avenue, Central Park.

At last, the ringing stops, and he peels his eyes open.

"I need a top-off," Mother slurs and holds up a glass of ice. It's midmorning, and Mother is deep in another rum and Coke bender. "We're out of Coke. Go to the cellar and get me some more."

Otis screams internally but keeps his face neutral. "We can't be out. I put a case in the refrigerator last night."

"You didn't. You promised me you would, but you didn't."

He did bring the case of soda up from the cellar. At least, he's pretty sure he did. They were watching *Wheel of Fortune* when she asked. "In a few minutes," he says. "I'm packing. The taxi will be here soon."

Mother scoffs and shakes her glass. The rattling ice is better than the godforsaken bell, but not much. "You don't have two minutes for your mother? I thought I raised you better. I'll do it myself, then. Don't you worry about me. I can handle those steep stairs."

Otis holds back a grimace and imagines Mother thumping down the cellar stairs one step at a time, her arthritic knees and ankles throbbing. "Don't be like that. I'll do it in a bit. I just need to finish packing. I don't want to be late to the airport."

Mother glares at him with her moist blue eyes. She's been in a foul mood since she failed to talk him out of his trip. Last night, she pleaded and cried and swore something terrible would happen to her if he left. A burglar would break in and slit her throat. She'd slip in the bathtub. The house would burn down around her. Her begging almost worked. She is an old woman who needs support. But he needs to escape, even if it's just for a few short days. It'd be good for the both of them.

After what feels like an eon, Mother maneuvers her wheelchair toward the living room instead of the kitchen and the cellar door. Seconds later, the TV turns on and he's treated to her favorite soap opera. A character Otis has a passing familiarity with is sleeping with another character's wife.

Back in his bedroom, he pulls a blue dress shirt and a brown sports coat from his closet. "I'm so glad I came," he says to the empty room. "The people make me feel so alive. People back home would never understand."

Mother's handbell drags him back to reality. She's impatient as always. With Mother, everything must be now. He pinches the bridge of his nose. *How is this my life? What happened?*

"Almost finished!" he shouts. Under his breath, he adds, "Then you can drink all the damned Coke you want. You can drown in it for all I care."

He finishes packing and stares out his bedroom window at the red barn he used to play in as a child. This time tomorrow, he'll be admiring skyscrapers from his hotel window. He's waited his whole life for this.

A shrill scream pierces the air, and Otis's heart rattles in his chest. A chill rushes over him. He darts out of his bedroom and down the steps toward Mother's shrieks. The living room is empty. He lingers for a moment before hurling himself into the kitchen. Mother's wheelchair sits empty in front of the cellar door.

She wouldn't, he thinks. But he knows Mother would if she's angry enough and drunk enough. Maneuvering around the wheelchair, he steps into the doorframe and gasps. Mother lies twisted at the bottom of the stairs, one arm trapped under her slight frame, her dress bunched around her shriveled thighs. Blood pours from her nose and down her lips.

When she sees him, she wails and rings her handbell harder. "Why did you do this to me?"

The soda machine spits Otis's dollar out for the third time, and he's forced once again to smooth the bill along the edge of the dispenser. "Just take it," he murmurs, inserting the dollar. This time, the machine accepts his cash. He punches the button for a Coke and snatches the can from the tray. More than two hours have passed since Mother was admitted to the hospital, and every muscle in his body, from his calves to his shoulders, is tight with worry.

"Mr. Ferryman?" a woman asks from behind.

He turns to the woman. She's short with thick-rimmed, plastic glasses and curly blonde hair pulled back in a neat ponytail. Her hooped earrings sparkle in the fluorescent light.

"Yes," Otis replies.

"My name is Dr. Mueller. I've just spoken with your mother. She asked me to speak with you, too."

"It's bad, isn't it?" he blurts out.

"No, nothing like that. Your mother didn't break any bones. She has deep contusions on her right arm and shoulder. She'll be sore for a few weeks, but she'll recover."

Otis's shoulders sag with relief, but some of the tension remains. "Are you certain? She was screaming something fierce when she came in."

"I'm certain," Dr. Mueller says. "Will you come with me, please?" She leads him through the corridors to a small room. Mother smiles as he enters, and he tries his hardest not to look away. The right side of her face is purplish and swollen. Dried flakes of blood from her split lip and busted nose stain the collar of her dress. Most distressing, her right arm is in a sling.

"Where did you go?" Mother asks, and Otis knows she's speaking to him. "You were gone so long. I had to send the doctor to find you."

"I was gone for just a few minutes, Mother." He pops open the can of Coke and hands it to her. "I got this for you."

"You're sweet," Mother says, then to Dr. Mueller, "See how sweet my boy is?" She takes a polite sip and hands the can back.

Dr. Mueller nods in acknowledgment, and Otis feels a little burst of approval jolt through him. Mother likes it when he's thoughtful; she likes it more when he's thoughtful around other people.

"I've told your mother this," Dr. Mueller says, "but she insisted I tell you as well. She needs to rest for the next few days. No strenuous activity. I've prescribed medication for her pain."

Mother reaches out with her good arm and takes Otis's hand. "Don't worry, Dr. Mueller, my baby boy will take care of me. He always takes good care of me."

"Mother, please." He hates it when she calls him that. *Baby boy.* He's a grown man. Has been for more than a decade. Why she continues to treat him like a child, he'll never know. Gently but firmly, he pulls his hand away.

A smile touches Dr. Mueller's lips. "I'm sure he will. If there's nothing else, you're free to go." She gives a quick nod to Otis and leaves.

As soon as she's out of sight, his anxiety rises again. He wants to follow Dr. Mueller and ask the question that's been nagging at the back of his mind since he arrived at the hospital. "I'll be right back, Mother," he says, rushing after the doctor. He catches her turning a corner toward the nurses' station. "Dr. Mueller, one moment, please."

She turns around slowly, and he realizes then that Dr. Mueller is the same age as him, maybe even younger. *How is she a doctor already?* he thinks with a hint of jealousy. He forces the thought away. "Thanks for dealing with Mother.

She can be…" he pauses, uncertain what to say, so he adds, "She's just set in her ways, that's all."

"She was no trouble, honestly. Can I help you?"

"Yes," he says, instinctually rubbing his cheek, a nervous reaction he's never been able to break. He bites his tongue, his mind roiling. Enough time passes that Dr. Mueller raises an eyebrow. *Just do it all at once!* his mind screams. Then, aloud: "Is there any way to tell if Mother threw herself down the stairs on purpose?"

Dr. Mueller tilts her head and her welcoming smile fades. She removes her glasses and slides them into her coat pocket. "Not that I know of. Are you telling me your mother threw herself down the stairs?"

"No, no," he stammers. "I'm not suggesting she did, but I want to be certain."

Dr. Mueller steps closer. She smells subtly of daisy and jasmine, and her closeness excites him as much as it makes him uncomfortable. "Mr. Ferryman, do you believe your mother might harm herself?"

He retreats back, putting as much distance between them as possible without seeming rude. *What would happen if I said yes? Would she take Mother away? Do I care?*

"Otis, where are you?" Mother shouts. "I want to go home."

Mother's voice drives the thoughts from his mind, and for a moment, he's filled with shame. She *is* his responsibility.

He forces a smile and looks Dr. Mueller in the eyes. "Mother calls. Just forget I said anything. I have an overactive imagination. That's what Mother says." He wheels around and jogs toward Mother. "Coming!"

"Fetch my bell, baby boy," Mother says as she eases into her recliner in the living room. Otis is at her side, steadying her. Once settled, she sighs with relief and pats his hand. He had hoped she'd forgotten about the bell, but no such luck. He's going to hear its head-splitting ring constantly over the coming weeks.

"Can I get you anything else?" he asks in a soft, placating voice.

With her good hand, she points to the remote on the coffee table, and he retrieves it for her. She flips the TV on and surfs, settling on a courtroom reality show he's unfamiliar with. "I want a rum and Coke. To help with the pain."

He grimaces with concern. That's the last thing she needs. "You really shouldn't, Mother. You're taking painkillers."

"I know what's good for me," she snaps back. "You're being nasty. No one likes a nasty boy. Go on and do what I say."

"Mother, please."

"Otis, stop arguing and just do it. I've had a long day. Would you deny your mother this one small thing?"

He bites his tongue. He won't win this fight. Either he makes Mother a drink, or she'll do it herself, and hers will be all rum. "Okay," he says, trying hard not to sound annoyed, and goes to the kitchen.

The door to the cellar is open, and the light is still on. Moving deliberately, he examines each step on his way down for splinters and jagged edges, anything that might have tripped Mother. There's nothing out of the ordinary, though.

The concrete floor at the bottom of the steps is another story. A small pool of partially congealed blood catches the light and his attention. It's barely the size of his palm but feels as expansive as the sky. Squatting, he pokes the blood, then rolls it between his thumb and index finger, and feels a surge of...satisfaction? He's not sure how to describe it. He doesn't want Mother to be in pain, but sometimes she needs to be reminded that she's an old woman, not God. Using a damp paper towel, he mops up the blood, then hunts for Mother's handbell.

It's difficult to remember precisely what happened after he found Mother in the cellar. He was moving too fast to commit everything to memory, but he thinks he kicked the handbell at some point.

It's a short search. He finds the bell under a row of wooden shelves crammed with canned fruits and vegetables and everything else they don't have space for in the upstairs cupboard. Picking it up, he feels a mix of reverence and disgust and is reminded that the bell is deceptively heavy and would make a dangerous weapon.

"I hate you," he whispers to the bell, imagining all the ways he could destroy it. All it would take is a few hard blows with a hammer. Or he could go for a ride in his truck and toss it out the window. A smile creeps across his lips, then drops. No matter what he did to the handbell, Amelia would find out and replace it. Maybe with one that's worse. Better to stick with the devil you know.

Moving on, he scans the shelves for the bright red case of Coke. When he doesn't find it, he steps back and rubs his cheek. If he didn't bring it upstairs last night, it should be here. *What the hell is happening?*

Confused and annoyed, he thumps up the cellar stairs, Mother's bell hanging limply at his side. He flings open the refrigerator and is only half surprised when he sees the case isn't there either. *It should be here unless someone moved it*, he thinks. *Unless Mother moved it.*

He closes the refrigerator and leans against it. Why would Mother move the case? It doesn't make sense. What was she planning? The answer hits a second later and a spike of anger devours him.

That witch!

When he was a teenager, Mother would sometimes drink too much and convince herself that he was going to leave her. She'd lure him into a room and lock him inside. He spent hours locked in his bedroom or the bathroom—and one time in the basement.

Fuming, he yanks open the cupboard door and eyes the shelves—nothing. He keeps going, checking all the places the case might be. It's not with the plates or Tupperware. It's not under the sink or with the pots and pans. He even checks the stove. Certain it's not in the kitchen, he moves to the dining room, spies the hutch. The case is shoved deep into the back, a bath towel draped over it.

"What's taking so long?" Mother hollers.

Otis storms into the living room, Mother's handbell in one hand, the case of Coke in the other. He's hot all over like he's just finished mowing the lawn on a scorching summer day.

"What was your plan?" he snarls and dumps the Cokes onto the hardwood floor. They bounce and roll in all directions. A single can bursts and hisses sweet, brown liquid into the air.

Mother's eyes go wide, and Otis knows he's caught her.

"I don't know what you're talking about," she says.

"You're a liar." It's all he can do to keep from shouting. "You hid them, so I'd go to the cellar to get more."

"You're not making sense," Mother says. "I don't like you when you're like this." She stands on wobbly legs and creaks to her wheelchair beside her recliner. "Take me to my room. I don't want to be around you."

Otis clenches his fists so hard his body shakes. "You were going to lock me down there, so I'd miss my flight, weren't you? And then you panicked because the taxi was almost here and—" He pauses and takes a seething breath. "You threw yourself down the steps."

"I'd never," Mother barks. "Of course, you'd blame me. It's your fault, Otis. It's your fault I hurt my arm and hurt my face. You did this to me. Ungrateful child. Do you know what I've done for you?"

He swallows hard and tries to calm himself. He can't. He feels the chains of Mother's needs. They tie him to Pulaski, the small county he can't escape; they tie him to this ancient house; they tie him to the same room he's lived in since he was born; they tie him to a life he doesn't want.

"Did you do it?" he demands, his voice rising to a shout.

"Why would you ask me that?" Mother asks and starts to cry.

He's seen Mother's tears a hundred thousand times, and they always break his heart. But he won't give in. She knew how important this trip was to him and didn't care.

She threw herself down the stairs to hurt him. He leans over her, his mood darkening. "Did you do it?"

Something changes in Mother when he doesn't immediately back down. She goes hard and wipes tears from her cheeks with two precise swipes. "Move," she says, trying to wheel around him to leave the room.

He blocks her. "You didn't want me to leave! It was a vacation, Mother! A single trip! One lousy week!"

She points a bony, clawed finger at him. "I didn't want you to go. That terrible city, with all those dirty people and their immoral thoughts, isn't for you."

"You don't know that!"

Mother tilts her head and smirks. "I know my baby boy. That city would have broken you. Just look at yourself, Otis. You can't take care of yourself."

Truth is a weapon, and Mother uses it like a bludgeon. He winces because deep in his heart, he knows she's right. A nobody in high school. A community college dropout. Fired from his first (and only) job. He's almost thirty-two years old and receives an allowance, money given to him from Mother's family inheritance.

"You're the most selfish person I know," he says, though the words are barely more than mumbles. Yet, as they stutter out, he feels a deep relief; they strengthen him. He needed to say this for a long time. "I wish you were dead!"

Mother's expression softens. She's on the verge of tears again. He doesn't care. He doesn't want to speak to her. He doesn't want to be in the same house as her, much less in the same room.

"Here's your bell," he says, tossing it on the floor.

Otis startles awake. His room is pitch black, except for a sliver of moonlight that bisects an old woven rug. Mother's shouting voice reaches him, full of panic. He jumps to his feet and hurries to her room on the first floor. Halfway there, she shouts again, and this time, he understands what she's yelling.

"Get out!" Mother screams. "Get out of here!"

Ready to fight, he throws himself through her bedroom door. He scans the room but relaxes when he realizes Mother's alone. She's in front of an open window, bracing herself on the frame. "Thieves! Trespassers! I see you! I know you're there!"

He joins her. Goose flesh ripples down his arms and across his chest as the night air touches his bare skin. "What are you going on about?"

Mother totters and points at the red barn across the yard. "Go on, take a look."

A bright violet light glows from behind the building. It takes a moment for Otis's mind to catch up to what he's seeing. Nothing is on that side of the barn but ankle-high grass. Fifty yards beyond the barn is a thick tree line that blocks both the barn and the house from the road. The light shouldn't be there, and there's only one explanation: someone's on their property.

He leans out the window and, in his deepest voice, shouts, "If you don't leave, I'm coming out there!" A couple of seconds pass, but the owner of the light stays silent. "You hear me! I'm going to come out there! You'll be sorry!"

When he's certain the trespassers aren't going to leave, he mutters a series of curses. Between missing his trip to New York, Mother's "fall," and now this, he's had it with today.

"Stay here," he tells Mother.

"Don't go," she replies.

"I'll be fine."

He snatches an aluminum baseball bat from the umbrella stand next to the front door and rushes outside. He's positive he's going to find a couple of kids drinking warm Milwaukee's Best and spray-painting penises on the side of the building. Near the barn, he slows to a stop and listens. The night is filled with noises: the hoot of owls and the chirp of crickets—but no voices.

"I know you're there," he shouts. "I can see your light. Get out of here before I call the cops." He waits for the kids to scatter, but nothing happens. "You hear me?"

More nothing.

Fear rolls up his spine and he rubs his cheek. Maybe his anger *has* gotten the best of him. What if the kids are waiting for him? He's read about the knockout game. Sure, it hasn't happened in Pulaski. But this could be the start of a spree. He could be this gang's first victim.

On a good day, he tops out at a cool five feet six inches and a buck forty. He also hasn't worked out since high school gym class. *What was I thinking?* He should have called the police already. Mother always said his temper would get the best of him. And she's right. It's another thing he hates her for. But it's too late now; he's already committed.

He raises the bat high and launches himself toward the barn at a full sprint. An incoherent scream bursts from his throat. As he rounds the corner to the far side of the barn, he stumbles, shocked at what he sees.

A white, wall-like object a little larger than the hood of a car and as thin as paper floats perpendicular to the barn. A violet glow pulses from within. Heart pounding in his ears, he sways to the side and leans against the barn to keep from collapsing. His hand goes slack, and the bat drops to the grass, barely making a sound.

The object, whatever it is, shouldn't exist. He lets out a soft moan and loses his senses. An eternity passes before he regains control of his body and can support himself without needing the barn. "Be brave," he murmurs as he retrieves his bat. *This is your home. You need to know what is happening.*

Holding the bat like a prod, he inches closer to the object. The smell of honey and rot assaults his nostrils. Close up, the object's white exterior reminds Otis of a damp, fragile membrane. Ever so gently, he presses the head of the bat into the object's center, expecting to penetrate it, only its exterior is elastic and bends around the bat.

Undeterred, he pushes harder and the bat punches through the object's moist surface with a stomach-twisting squelch. A viscous, milky discharge dribbles out of the hole and down the face of the object. He pulls the bat out with ease and examines the goo sliding down the shaft toward his bare hand. Before it can touch him, he flings the bat aside and returns his focus to the object. The hole he punched in it is healing itself.

"Fuck me," he says over and over, each time softer than the last until finally, he's mouthing the words. *What have I found? What do I do with it?*

A frantic ringing grabs his attention. Mother is going wild with her handbell. She's been waiting for him to come back all this time and probably thinks he's been hurt, or worse. He needs to deal with her first, then...*the object, the membrane, the opening*. He can't decide what to call it, so they'll all have to do for now.

Hustling, he jogs around the barn into the front yard. Mother is still hanging out her window. "Everything is okay!" he says, waving a hand overhead. "You can go back to bed." He's unsure what to make of the object, but he's certain he doesn't want Mother involved.

"What's going on?" she asks. "Are there kids out there?"

"No kids."

"I'm calling the police."

"Don't, I'll do it." It's a miracle she doesn't argue.

Back inside the house, he takes up the cordless phone in the living room and steps into the dining room, where he closes the sliding doors so Mother can't hear the conversation.

He punches the first number for 9-1-1 into the phone, then stops. What if the operator doesn't believe him? Ryan Cooke, an acquaintance from high school, called the police because he saw a hairless gray monster with three long fingers while walking home from Hap's Bar one night. Ryan is three years sober now, but the story will stay with him until he dies. That's life in a small town. If Otis calls this in, he's setting himself up for a lifetime of gossip. It can't be helped, though. What's out behind the barn is real; he touched it.

He dials the second number and pauses again. Something else will happen, too. The government will get involved. Sheriff Hayes is going to come out here and then the army. He's watched enough movies to know how it goes. They'll take the object from him. Does he want that? No, he doesn't think so. The object could be valuable. He might be a community college dropout, but he's not stupid. The object is unique, and unique sells.

This could be my way out. The thought pops into his head like a lightning strike. *I've wanted a way out for so long.* In his mind, he sees himself in New York and L.A. and London. He sees the small house where he'll live. There's a dog, too, because Mother can't stand pets and won't let him have one. His finger hovers over the one button but doesn't press it again. Instead, he ends the call with a hard push of his thumb and sets the phone on the dining room table.

The fear flowing through him disappears, and hope takes its place. The object is valuable. His story is valuable. He can sell his story, and with the money he makes, he can escape Pulaski and the drafty old house he's lived in his whole life.

He can escape Mother.

It's not even noon, and Otis is lathered in sweat. Bits of dirt cling to his jeans and untucked white T-shirt, and his hands and arms are streaked with dust. He hasn't worked this hard in a long time, not since Mother asked him to put in a vegetable garden behind the house.

It's safe now, he thinks to himself as he admires the ramshackle shed he's built around the glowing opening. Roughly square, the shed is a collection of warped plywood, wooden pallets, and cheap pressed wood from a discarded bookshelf. Instead of a door, two paint-splattered drop cloths dangle from the roof. The shed is ugly as sin and clashes with the red barn, but he doesn't care like he usually would. What's important is that the wall is hidden from curious kitties like Amelia and everyone else in Pulaski like her.

Satisfied with his work, he pulls the drop cloths over the entrance. The only sign of the object inside is the violet light peeking through the structure's seams. He'll come back later with duct tape to cover the holes. Right now, he needs a shower.

Before heading to the house, he stops to pocket the digital camera sitting in the grass beside the barn. It's filled with two dozen pictures of the opening from various distances and angles. They're his proof in case something happens to it. As he rounds the corner, he sees Mother sitting quietly on the porch, glowering at him, a highball glass at her lips. She's on her way to another bender. *Here we go.*

Mother is still angry with him for accusing her of throwing herself down the stairs. And when she's angry, she uses her favorite weapon to punish him—silence. She'll ignore him until he apologizes. She can carry on like this for days. Once, she didn't speak to Otis for a month.

He forces himself to smile and waves at Mother. Inside, he's angry with himself for how much her silent treatment hurts him. Lord knows he's tried to not let it bother him, but it always does. After Father left, it was the two of them against Pulaski. And when Otis was bullied by his classmates, she put a stop to it and held him close as he cried himself to sleep. That has to count for something.

Mother doesn't wave back. Big surprise. She drains her highball, places the glass on the small table next to her, and starts to creep toward the front door. With her right arm in a sling, she can't use her hands to propel her wheelchair. To get around this, she uses her feet to turn the wheelchair so its back faces the door and pushes herself to the entrance. With a little grunt, she flings open the screen door and tries to get herself inside. Before she makes it, the screen snaps back in place.

"I'll get it for you," Otis calls out. He double-times to the porch and motions for her to move away from the screen, which she reluctantly does. He pulls the screen door open, and she awkwardly kicks herself inside. The whole time, she's forced to face him, and instead of looking directly at him, she stares at the barn. She looks old and tired today, unlike her usual self and more like the person she actually is—a woman in her early sixties in poor health. The pungent smell of rum trails behind her, and he knows she's drunk again. She rolls into the living room and clicks on the TV.

"You should eat," Otis says as he heads to the kitchen. He hopes some food will soak up the alcohol in her system and keep her from passing out in front of her soaps. "Do you want a sandwich? I'm going to make a sandwich."

Mother replies by turning up the volume on the TV to drown him out. Today, a panel of women are arguing about when adult children should live with their parents. If Amelia were here, she'd have already taken a potshot at him about it.

A few minutes later, he sets up Mother's aluminum TV tray and presents her with a turkey sandwich made just how she likes it: extra tomatoes, light on the mayo. He adds a glass of iced sweet tea. "Here you go."

He settles into the sofa and takes a bite of his own sandwich. Food tastes better when you've worked for it, and that's what he's done today. "What are you watching?" he asks, just to make conversation.

He gets a different response this time. Mother makes a noise that's somewhere between a grunt and a snort, and flips through the channels as fast as possible. A cacophony of truncated words and music attacks the room.

"Okay, you have a good afternoon," he says, climbing off the couch. "Ring if you need anything." She won't, not unless it's an emergency.

He goes to his room on the second floor and showers. Feeling human again, he fires up his Dell. Building the shed was only the first step in his plan. Now, he needs to learn more about the object. He pulls up Google and searches for "real glowing portal." The top searches are related to a bunch of video games he's never heard of.

He tries "holes in reality" next but is more disappointed in the results than in his first attempt. All of the websites he finds are about black holes. Which, to be fair, he's curious about, but they don't match the description of the pulsing opening in his front yard.

Next, he searches for "large glowing orb," "magic doorways," "wormholes," and a dozen others. He's on the verge of quitting when he remembers the countless crime shows he's watched with Mother over the years and decides to focus on the *who* instead of the *what*. A few keystrokes later, he comes across a reference to something called the Hawthorn Incident where three people disappeared after discovering a "vibrating white opening."

His heart slams in his throat when he follows the backlink and lands on an article with the title, "Investigating the Hawthorn Incident" that recounts the disappearance of retirees John and Kat Hawthorn and their neighbor Darius Haskins.

According to the site, John and Kat discovered an ooze-filled opening in a field about fifteen miles outside of Libby, Montana, that they called a "dimensional tear." After studying it for a short time, they decided to explore inside with their neighbor. All three disappeared, but they left behind detailed notes, photographs, and a jar of viscous, cloudy liquid. The author of the article, a woman named Cherry Raven, speculated the trio disappeared after the opening closed with them inside it.

Leaning back in his chair, he rubs his cheek. He doesn't trust the article, not wholly. Who has a name like Cherry Raven? A made-up name, for sure. And yet, there are remarkable similarities between the Hawthorn's dimensional tear and whatever is in his shed.

In the long run, though, he doesn't give a damn *what* is on the other side of the opening, so long as *something* is there. A verdant, untouched paradise? Great. A barren rock? Great too. What matters is what comes after he shares the opening's existence with the rest of the world.

He'll be on the cover of *People* and interviewed on *Good Morning America*. Somewhere down the line, he'll write a biography. When he's older, of course, and has more to tell. The book will succeed—number one in *The New York Times*. Hell, he'd settle for landing in the top ten. He's not greedy.

He shuts off the monitor. Between not sleeping and building the shed, he's dog-tired and needs a nap. Mother says only lazy people sleep the day away, but he's earned a rest. Besides, how often has he seen her passed out in the afternoon? He can't begin to guess.

Settling into bed, he closes his eyes but can't sleep. His brain is worked up and firing question after question at him. *Is the shed good enough? What if the opening disappears? What if Amelia sees the opening? Who will she tell?*

Then a terrifying thought washes over him—*What will happen to Mother?* He can't leave her alone in Pulaski. Who would take care of her? Not Amelia. Sure, she'd swing by a few times a week to gossip, but she wouldn't mow the grass or shop for groceries. She can't carry Mother to bed when her legs hurt so bad she can't walk.

He jolts up and pads to his desk. His old chair creaks as he eases into it. Slowly, he slides his palm against the underside of the desk until he finds the key he's hidden. Years ago, when Mother was healthier, he discovered that when he left the house, she'd climb the steps to the second floor and search his room. Sometimes, he thinks she still does.

He unlocks the desk and opens the bottom drawer. His plane ticket to New York rests on top of his most private possessions. Seeing the ticket makes him boil with rage; he pulls it out and taps it against his forehead while telling himself he'll have another chance to travel to the Big Apple. *Soon.*

He sets the ticket aside and removes a vintage nudie mag he bought at a garage sale when he was twelve. He still can't believe the old man sold it to him, but he's thankful for the perv. One layer lower is a notebook filled with poetry he wrote to Camilla Clarke, the girl he dated senior year. Mother put a stop to that. She said her baby boy was too good for a harlot.

A bulbous purple and yellow action figure is wedged in the corner. It's the last of his childhood toys. Mother threw the others away when he turned nine. She only missed this one because he brought it to school that day. Setting it aside, he eyes the only remaining object left in the drawer, a white envelope. His stomach roils looking at it, and he stifles a gag when he picks it up. Inside is a trifold brochure for Creekside Assisted Living.

Mother is slumped in her recliner, snoring softly. Otis shuts the TV off and swats at a fly circling her untouched sandwich. In the kitchen, he tosses the food in the trash and empties what's left of her latest rum and Coke in the sink. He knows what he has to do but doesn't want to go through with it. He can hear Mother's screams and sobs in his mind. He can see her calling him a naughty child, cursing him, and weakly slapping his chest.

"It has to happen," he whispers to the kitchen. Hearing the words out loud bolsters his resolve. He loves Mother and wants her to be safe and taken care of—but if he doesn't get out of this house and live his own life, something terrible will happen.

Something *more terrible* will happen.

He doesn't need to be cruel, though. He's better than that. He's better than Mother.

Forty something years ago, Rebecca Ferryman was crowned Ms. Pulaski County three years running. *The Pulaski Times*, the county's local newspaper, dedicated its front page to her wins. He's read every word of the story a thousand times; he even did a report about Mother's wins in fourth grade when his teacher asked the class to profile a local celebrity.

In the column, Henry Peterman, the paper's editor-in-chief, detailed Mother's beauty in the most purple of purple prose. "Her hair is the color of cool shade in a burning August sun." The man's writing is too lecherous for Otis, but Mother loves it. And he has to admit that Mother was uncommonly attractive. The pictures accompanying the column are of a young woman, exuberant and laughing, one hand clutching her chest in surprise. He wishes a trace of that young woman existed in Mother today. Maybe things would be different between them. Jealousy is there, too; Mother has accomplished so much more in her life than him.

Near the end of the article, there is a quote from Mother that always makes him roll his eyes. When asked what she attributed to her multiple wins, Mother points to her strict diet. "I'll eat anything, but not everything."

This is true—for the most part. Mother is a violent eater. During meals, she doesn't so much eat her food as dissect it to find a few palatable bites. When it comes to sweets, however, all bets are off. She has a sweet tooth that would kill a honeybee. Soda, sweet tea, candy bars, cinnamon rolls, cherry pie—she loves them all. She'll devour every crumb and ask for more. Her absolute favorite sweet—the thing that makes her happier than anything else in the world—is simple yellow cake with buttercream frosting.

For years now, he's baked Mother a yellow cake for her birthday. Not from a box, mind you. He does it all from scratch because it's what Mother wants from him: time, sweat, devotion. Everything a good son must give freely to his mother. Tonight, he'll give her all these things one more time. He can do that much for her before he breaks her heart.

Three hours later, the cake is ready. It's round and two tiers tall with half an inch of white butter frosting. *My best one yet*, Otis thinks, as he covers it with a glass dome—the same thought he has every time he makes one.

Out in the living room, the TV blares. Mother is awake again, watching an old black-and-white movie by the sound of it. He's heard her moving about, but they haven't seen or spoken to each other. She's probably dying for another rum and Coke. It must be nice to go through life in a haze, having someone else care for you.

He's aggressively scrubbing flour and sugar off his forearms when the doorbell rings. Mother won't answer the door, not unless she's expecting Amelia. He beelines from the kitchen into the dining room and pushes the sliding divider doors open. Through the front door window, he spots an annoyed young man in a white button-down shirt and slicked-back hair. Otis recognizes the face instantly, and his chest swells with pride. It's not every day you can convince Pauline's Italian Bistro—Pulaski's best restaurant—to ignore their no-takeout policy and send a server out to deliver food.

Otis steps outside and is shocked by how late in the day it is. The sun has set and remaining gray light is rapidly fading. He gently pulls the door shut behind him. "It's a surprise," he says in a low voice, hoping Garth—their regular waiter at the restaurant—is smart enough to mimic him and keep his voice down. "Thank you again for coming all this way. Mother isn't feeling well. This will lift her spirits."

"Anything for Mrs. Ferryman. She's our best customer," the man replies as he places two brown bags on the porch. By the tone of his voice, Otis knows Garth is being polite.

Otis counts out cash for the bill and adds a hefty tip. He thanks Garth again before slipping back into the dining room and closing the sliding doors. It doesn't take long to set the table and dispose of the food containers. The room is replete with the rich, semi-acidic aroma of red sauce and garlic.

Looking over Mother's special meal, he feels a flaming ball of distress ascend from his stomach to the back of his throat. He is fear and trepidation personified. *I can do this*, he thinks, rubbing his cheek with his middle knuckles. *This is what's best for both of us. She knows it, too.*

"Raise the curtains," he says and opens the sliding doors that lead to the living room.

Mother pays him no mind when he steps into the room. "Dinner is ready," he says. The words are barely out of his mouth before she cranks the TV volume to full. His back jaw tightens, but her childishness won't stop him. He maneuvers around the furniture and blocks the TV with his body. "Dinner is ready," he shouts over the movie.

Mother's lips draw tight, and she flicks her wrist at him, the universal sign for *get the hell out of the way*. Undaunted, he whips around and yanks the TV plug from the wall. The room goes silent. Mother's eyes narrow, and her nostrils flair.

"It's time to eat," he says softly, forcing as much contrition into his voice as possible. It's what she wants, and he doesn't want to drag this out more. All he needs to do is get Mother into the dining room. "Mother, it's special."

A beat passes, and when he knows she won't answer him, he crosses the room and gently pulls her to a standing position. Instead of slapping him, as he expected, she goes half-limp, forcing Otis to hold her up. It's times like these that he's grateful Mother is such a petite wisp of a woman. He gently places Mother into her wheelchair and rolls her to the dining room table.

"This is for you," he says eagerly. A glass of white wine is already waiting for her. Another is chilling in the refrigerator. By the end of dinner, he plans to be drunk.

He takes his place at Mother's side, and before she speaks, he gulps down half of his own glass of wine. It chills his insides and bubbles his mind. Seconds tick past, but Mother doesn't say a word. Her posture is tense as she studies the meal. At half a minute, the urge to rub his cheek threatens to overwhelm Otis, and he knows deep down that he's screwed up. She doesn't like any of these. He raises his hand, catches himself, and then drops it under the table, where he clutches his jeans. When he was young, Mother would smack the back of his hand with a wooden spoon if she caught him doing it. "Don't you like it?" he asks.

Mother turns her icy blue eyes to him, and he instinctively shrinks into himself. She's going to shout at him and tell him everything he's done wrong. She's going to break him with her words. With a slow inhale, he prepares himself. *Go ahead, try to break me. I have a secret. I have a future.*

"You did this for me?" Mother asks in a flat tone. Then, a smile cracks her lips, and the tension in the room lessens. Under the table, he stretches his fingers, the urge to rub his cheek gone. "You're so sweet."

"I thought this would make you feel better."

"This goes a long way, baby boy."

Otis serves chicken francese and steamed broccoli. Before he gives Mother her plate, he cuts the meat into small pieces. The whole while, she watches approvingly, luxuriating in the attention. He does the same for his own chicken, and together, they push and shove their food back and forth on their plates. Mother is hunting for her perfect bite, but he has no appetite. What he is, though, is thirsty.

He pours himself a second glass of wine and takes another drink.

"We need to talk about yesterday, Mother," he says halfway through the meal. "I know you didn't throw yourself down the stairs. I'm sorry." It's a necessary lie, he reassures himself.

"Good. I know I didn't raise a foolish boy," Mother says. "To think you thought I'd hurt myself just to keep you from going to see that filthy city. You should have gone anyway. I would have been fine on my own."

Otis's stomach crumbles into itself, and his mouth goes dry. He takes a sip of his wine to calm his anger, and when it's not enough, he sucks down the whole glass. "We need to talk about your health. It's not safe for you to live here anymore."

Mother goes rigid, then, with exaggerated care, places her fork on top of her meal. "I'm old enough to make my own decisions. I'm also your mother. You can't tell me what to do."

From his back pocket, Otis pulls out the pamphlet for Creekside Assisted Living and slides it across the table to Mother. She lets it lay halfway between them. "I've visited.

It's a nice facility. You'd like it there. They can take care of you better than I can."

Mother's forehead creases and her jaw hardens. "How dare you? You want to toss me out like an old dress! You want to ball me up and throw me away. I won't go! I refuse to go!"

"It's not like that, and you know it," he says. "You can't take care of yourself. Look at your arm. What if I hadn't been here when you fell? How long would you have laid there? Hours? Days? What would you have done?"

"I would have been fine." She shoves her plate away so hard that it slams into the candelabra at the center of the table, knocking it over. Flames lick at the white tablecloth, blackening it.

Otis jumps up and douses the small fire with a glass of water before it can grow. "You did that on purpose! Are you happy with yourself?"

"We're finished with this conversation," Mother says. "Clear my plate. It was terrible."

What a mess, Otis thinks, barely managing to stop himself from telling her to go to Hell. He uses a napkin to soak up the water, then pours a third glass of wine and drains it.

"Next time, you should just drink it straight from the bottle."

"Oh, really? How many rum and Cokes do you drink a day? Five, six, a dozen?" Otis says, seething. "You're a drunk, Mother. You've been one my whole life, and if I were you, I'd drink too. You're a nasty woman."

He hears the words leave his mouth and regrets them immediately. He's backed her into a corner. Now, she'll never leave the house, just to spite him. In a rush, he blurts out, "I'm sorry, I didn't mean that. We don't have to fight. Please just think about what I said. That's all I'm asking you to do."

"I don't need to think about it," Mother replies. "I'm not leaving. You're a stupid child for thinking I would."

He fights the growing urge to rub his check and instead readjusts his glasses. He needs to clear the air, put everything that just happened behind him. He needs Mother to love him again, the way a mother should love a son. "I made something special for you."

"I don't want it," she says.

"You do. I know you do. Stay right there." He dashes to the kitchen and returns with the cake. "I made you your favorite dessert," he says, placing it on the table in front of her. He waits, suspended in anxiety, for her to speak.

"I don't like cake," Mother snaps. "I've never liked it. Take that thing away. I won't eat it. Especially not if you made it."

"It's your favorite. I've seen you eat it hundreds of times."

"Take it away and bring me a rum and Coke."

He ignores her and carefully cuts her a thick slice. "Just try it. Maybe you'll like it. Maybe it'll be your *new* favorite dessert."

"I don't want it." Locking eyes with him, Mother picks up the slice with her good hand. "You eat it," she says and smashes it into his face.

He gasps and stumbles back. The sweet taste of sugar rushes over his tongue, and for half a second he's blinded by the frosting. Using both hands, he digs the buttercream from his eyes and flings it to the ground.

"You're so unbelievably selfish!" he screams. "The only person you care about is yourself! That's why Father left. That's why everyone leaves!"

"And you're an ungrateful child!" Mother screams back. "You can't even support yourself. What type of man are you, living off your mother? You're just like your father. It's pathetic."

"Listen to me. You're going to Creekside whether you like it or not. I'll find a way, you understand me? I won't be your servant for the rest of my life. I won't do it. I can't do it."

Mother blubbers. He's never spoken to her this way before. When she recovers, she goes rigid and says, "Do it, and you'll never get another cent from me. Not one penny. That's all you want, anyway. You want to rob me blind and flitter away. You're just waiting for me to die."

"I don't need your money! I have my own now!"

Mother pulls back from him and cocks her head in surprise. She doesn't believe him. Why would she? Her eyes pierce him with hatred that he's only seen once before, the day Father left. Mother won't be silenced; she won't let a slight go unanswered. That is not who Regina Ferryman is; her nature defies compromise.

"I threw myself down the stairs on purpose!" she says. "I did it just to keep you here!" She raises her head as if she were being judged in a pageant. She's so proud of herself that it hurts him to look at her.

He already knew Mother intentionally hurt herself, but a small part of him hoped she hadn't. Because what proof did he have, really? Some hidden Coke cans? He wanted to believe Mother was better than that. Now he knows she's not. Tears well at the corners of his eyes. "You knew what that trip meant to me."

"We don't get what we want!" Mother shouts. "None of us do!"

"I will," he yells back, rage building inside him. He hates this old woman and how she's tethered him to this crappy little town, holding him back. How many years has he wasted on her? He needs her gone. Bending over so he's face-to-face with her, he says in a cold, razor-sharp voice he doesn't recognize, "I'll get it all. Everything I ever wanted. Starting today."

Mother goes pale. Unrecognizable words leak from her quivering lips. He doesn't care what she's trying to say. It's too late. If her tongue is still a bloody butcher knife, so what? She can't hurt him more than she already has.

Summoning his strength, he forces Mother into her wheelchair and pushes her out the front door into the night. "I have a secret I want to share with you," he says, picking up speed.

She hisses in pain from being jostled from side to side. "Take me back inside! Take me back now!"

Rounding the barn's corner, Otis spots the shed. Violet light shines from the holes he hasn't patched yet. He parks Mother in front of the shed and opens the drop cloths, revealing the glowing opening inside. Looking at it makes his body flush with excitement. Using his bare hands, he tears the object's membrane open. Sticky discharge coats his frosting-covered hands and slides down his forearms. Without the membrane, the violet light glows so bright that he's forced to look away. He returns to Mother's wheelchair and pushes her closer.

"Oh, God, Otis! What is that?" Mother cries.

"Your future," he says, and dumps her inside.

Finally, relief.

The weight of Otis's existence shifts, lightens. The world opens to him. He feels like a child who's been told he can be anything, can do anything. And Otis Ferryman can. He can do it all because he's unshackled from Mother's torment and hate.

Raising his fists high into the night, he howls. When his throat goes raw, he drops to his knees and then collapses to his back. His breath slows as he looks up at the night sky. Has it always been this beautiful? A smile spreads across his lips as he imagines his future. He's wasted so much time on Mother. His new life starts now.

He sits up and focuses on the opening. The membrane is closing, healing itself. Mother's wheelchair lays on its side in front of it. In that moment, his vision tunnels, and a terrible chill razors his spine. Reality snaps shut around him. He is a possum in a steel trap.

"Oh, God! What have I done?" He rubs his cheek for half a heartbeat before crawling through the prickly grass to the opening. It's right there in front of him, an inch away, pulsing greedily. He tells himself to go after Mother over and over again, but his body won't listen.

Trembling, he rises to his knees and cradles himself. *I don't know what's in there,* he thinks. *It could be dangerous. Mother wouldn't want me to follow if it's dangerous. I'm her baby boy.*

He lumbers across the front lawn toward the house. He's drunk. Why did he drink so much wine? It was just there, and he couldn't stop. He would have never hurt Mother if he were sober. Not a chance. *Tonight was an accident*, he tells himself. *Tempers were hot.*

Inside, he snatches up the phone from its cradle and prepares to call for help. *What will I say? I got drunk and threw my mother into—what, an opening? A gateway?* They'd lock him up. He rubs his cheek again. He's so soft. Not fit for prison. He'd die there.

But he must get help.

Then a stray thought cuts through his panic: *They'll take my discovery. They'll steal my future.* He drops the handset as if it were radioactive. It bounces off the rug and tumbles away. No one is taking his future from him; he's worked too hard for it.

He'll save Mother himself.

Otis pulls his old high school gym bag from under his bed. It's covered in dust and still smells of stale sweat all these years later. He doesn't even know why he kept it; he should have trashed it a long time ago, but he didn't. Maybe it's providence? Proof this was all meant to happen.

Downstairs, he stuffs the tote with mason jars filled with tap water, a box of Chewy Granola Bars, a blanket, and Mother's pain pills. The last items he adds are a half bottle of rum and three warm Cokes. If Mother is alive, he'd rather she be drunk and sedated than crawling around in agony.

Flashlight in hand, he trundles to the opening. Halfway there, his stomach sours, and he waters the lawn with chunky red vomit flecked with a pasta mush and masticated chicken. He wipes the burning upchuck from his nostrils and keeps going.

Nothing has changed since he left. The opening undulates and throbs, its violet light spilling into the world. Mother's wheelchair still lays on its side. "I'm here, Mother!" he cries out. "I'm sorry. I'm so, so sorry. Please, tell me you're okay."

He holds his breath and listens for her voice. All he hears are crickets trilling. He'd do anything to hear Mother scream at him, to call him a lay-about, an idiot, a failure. Painful words are better than no words. Thirty seconds pass without Mother calling back.

The tote's weight inches up his arm, urging him to act. "Mother, if you can hear me, I'm giving you supplies." He draws back from the opening and rushes forward with an underhand throw. The tote goes end over end and disappears into the violet glow.

"Stay where you are! I'll get you out. I promise."

Otis is on his hands and knees in the guest room closet, hunting for a box of old electronics. He finds it stuffed in the corner and drags it out. Digging through the box, he expects to find an ancient handheld camcorder that Father bought to record Mother's piano recitals.

"Come on," he growls when he discovers it's not there. In a last-ditch effort, he wrestles a wooden rocking chair from the corner of the room to the closet and climbs onto it. It's a terrible idea, but it's the best way to see what's stored on the shelf above him. Old baseball caps are on the left, and a cookie tin filled with sewing supplies is on the right. He pushes the hats to the side, and his heart jolts with excitement. The camcorder is stuffed in a leather bag on top of a shoebox that, if he remembers correctly, is filled with old family photos.

Legs shaking, he jumps off the rocking chair with the leather bag held tight to his chest. He lands awkwardly and slams into the hardwood. An image of Mother standing in front of the cellar door, ready to jump, flashes through his mind. How did she do it, knowing she'd hurt herself so badly? He could never go through with it himself. The pain would be too much.

He groans as he sits up and unzips the bag. Inside is the camcorder, battery, charger, and two cassettes. He plugs the battery into the device and thumbs the power button. Nothing happens. It's enough to make him scream.

He crawls to the nearest outlet and plugs the battery in. It'll take an hour, maybe two, for the camcorder to charge.

Stay calm, he tells himself, though his heart is rat-a-tat-tatting in his chest. *Mother is tough as nails.*

While he waits, he gathers a push broom from the hall closet, duct tape from a drawer in the kitchen, sunglasses from the dresser, and a jar of loose change from by the door. An excruciating hour later, he collects his new kit and stumble-runs back to the opening.

"I'm still here, Mother," he says, panting. "It's just going to take a little while longer."

He spins off the push broom's brush and tosses it aside. Then, with shaky hands, he tapes the jar of change to one end of the stick and the partially charged camcorder to the other, forming a combination prod and camera mount. He slips on the sunglasses. "God, please work," he whispers and presses the record button.

The opening's membrane isn't fully healed yet. One terrifying inch at a time, he pushes the camcorder inside. Without the membrane, there is little resistance. The hardest part is that even with sunglasses, the violent light sears his eyes.

With his heart assaulting his chest, he braces and carefully sweeps the camcorder back and forth, then up and down to capture as much of what's inside the opening as possible. Ninety seconds later, his arms start to tremble from exhaustion, and he pulls the camcorder from the opening. Like with his baseball bat, viscous goo drips off it. He envisions Mother lathered in the sticky substance, weeping for him.

Disgusting, he thinks. He doesn't want to touch the ooze again but forces himself to scoop as much of it as he can off the camcorder. Its texture reminds him of condensed milk. His heart sinks as he works. If he's captured anything at all, it'll be obscured by the discharge.

But he has to try. He has to look. He can't give up that easily. What would Mother say to him if he did? She'd be oh so disappointed, and she'd show him how she felt with a stern look and frown across her narrow face.

He peels the duct tape off the camcorder and jogs back to the house. In the living room, he hooks the camcorder to the TV and rewinds the cassette. Sitting cross-legged, camcorder in his lap, he presses the play button and leans toward the screen.

The image is gray and shapeless. As he suspected, everything is blurry from the goo on the lens. The only thing he's sure of is the camcorder's light. There is nothing else. He can't even see the source of the violet light leaking from the opening.

"Be there," he says in a threatening voice. He tries to wipe sweat from his brow but only accomplishes rubbing the sticky substance above his right eye. "I know you're there. Show me you're there."

The time stamp in the top right corner of the TV ticks up and up. Fifteen seconds. Thirty. Forty-five. Sixty. He holds his breath and mashes his back teeth together. He has to go inside now and search for Mother himself. Ninety seconds hit, and he watches his past self pull the camcorder out of the opening.

"Shit," he snaps, and rewinds the tape. He pumps the volume and presses play again. If he can't see Mother, maybe, if he's extremely lucky, he'll hear her.

Half a minute into the recording, there's nothing but muted white noise. Then, at the forty-two-second mark, he hears a faint whisper. His body shudders as he rewinds the tape to listen again.

Through the crackle, a woman asks, "Is that you?"

Mother would be proud.

Otis pauses to admire the rig he's engineered. His truck is backed up to the opening. A yellow nylon rope snakes from its hitch to Mother's wheelchair. If everything goes as planned, she'll be back with him in minutes.

"Step back, Mother," he shouts into the opening. He counts to ten and, with a back-aching grunt, tosses

Mother's wheelchair inside. Next to him, the yellow rope uncoils eight or nine feet before it stops. As he'd hoped, the rope is suspended in the center of the opening like exposed wire drooping from drywall. He re-ties the rope on his hitch to reduce slack, and then strings Mother's handbell to the center.

"Tug on the rope when you're ready. I'll pull you out."

A few minutes pass, but nothing happens, and his anxiety begins to creep upward. After ten minutes, he starts to pace the length of the rope line, his right hand gently stroking his cheek. He eyes Mother's infuriating handbell. *Ring, goddamn you!*

Somewhere around the forty-minute mark, he tells himself that he needs to be patient—unless he wants to go in himself. Which isn't happening.

An hour later, he pleads with Mother to strap herself to the chair. That's all she has to do. It's such a small thing. Hardly any effort at all. *Strap in. Ring the bell. I'm waiting. I'm waiting. I'm waiting.*

By dawn, he's on the verge of a breakdown that worsens when he realizes he's covered in filth. His shirt and pants are damp with sour sweat and cling to his chest and thighs. Dried puke and cake bits are encrusted around his collar. His forearms are scaly with desiccated discharge. This isn't how today was supposed to go. He was supposed to be in New York City, on Broadway, in a blazer, his hair oiled and parted with a perfect line.

I can't do this! He screams at himself. He stumbles to the house and throws open the front door with a bang. An unopened bottle of Bacardi rum is in the kitchen cabinet waiting for him. He hates the stuff, but it's stiff and right in front of him. It'll take the edge off, at least a little. Help him get through this. It's liquid courage, he knows, but it's still courage.

He removes the cap with a quick twist, and a sweet, oaky scent hits him. It reminds him of Mother. Why does everything in this forsaken house remind him of her? His throat burns as the liquor pours into his body. He takes a second swig, deeper this time, and drops to the floor, back to the wall. As the rum warms him, his throbbing hangover eases and his heart slows. He stays like this until his guilt forces him to move.

Bottle in hand, he returns to the opening and is met with more silence. He unlatches the tailgate of his truck, hops up, and takes another long pull of rum. Already, the world is blurry around the edges, and he feels good. If he stays like this, he can wait forever.

The sound of a car door closing startles Otis awake. Gasping, he sits up and almost slides off the tailgate. His mouth is dry, and his headache is back. It's early afternoon, and the sun's rays are strong enough that he feels like he's being judged. "Jesus," he says, realizing he fell asleep. *Why am I like this?*

He drops to the ground and kicks the empty rum bottle at his feet. He couldn't have drunk that much, but his memory is fuzzy. Edging around the truck, he checks to see who's calling. If he's lucky, it's the postman. He groans at what he sees. A pink Oldsmobile is parked in the driveway, and Amelia is plowing her way through the grass toward him. A sturdy woman with dyed light brown hair, she reminds him of an overly protective mutt.

"Otis, is that you?" she asks in her too-loud voice. He's known the woman his entire life, and he can't remember a time when she didn't sound like she was shouting.

Instead of answering, he pulls down the drop cloths to hide the opening. "Who else would it be?" he shouts back in his most jovial tone and hustles to stop her from coming too close to the shed.

Amelia waves her hand in front of his nose as he approaches. "Otis, you smell like a distillery. What's gotten into you?"

He ignores her. "Mother is asleep. I'll tell her to call you when she wakes up."

"I've been calling all morning, and no one's answered. I'm going to check on her. Someone needs to take care of her. I can't believe you let her fall down those stairs, Otis. Your head is always someplace else."

"I don't want you bothering Mother," he says, and blocks her path to the house.

"I know what Rebecca would want. I've known her for over fifty years. Move."

She attempts to step around him, but he grabs her by the fat of her arm. Her eyes go wide with disbelief. "This isn't your home, Amelia. You're going to leave. Mother is ill and doesn't want to be disturbed. Not by you, not by anyone. She doesn't care if Jesus Christ has come to carry her off to the Pearly Gates."

Amelia goes red, and she stammers. There is a good chance no one in Pulaski has ever denied Amelia King anything, and her shocked expression shows it. Like Mother, she comes from local royalty. "I... I... I have a mind to call the cops, Otis Ferryman. For all I know, you could be holding your mother hostage in there."

He exhales through his nose, his anger growing. "You'll feel silly when they arrive. They might cart you off for making a disturbance. Imagine spending the day in jail with all those criminals, those sinners you like to prattle on about. You'd be the talk of the town."

"I don't prattle," Amelia says, but there's no conviction behind her words. Her shoulders slump and she looks away. God forbid her name ends up in the local blotter. She'd never be able to show her face at church again. "I'm leaving, but only because I want to. Your mother is going to hear about this. I'm going to tell her how rude you were to her dearest friend. If you were my child, I'd put you over my knee, no matter your age."

"Then we're both lucky I'm not your child."

As Amelia pulls away, she scowls at him. She's a problem. She'll call and call, and when Mother doesn't answer, she'll snoop back unannounced and let herself inside with the spare key Mother gave her decades ago. He prays Mother will be back before it comes to that.

With Amelia gone, Otis returns his attention to the rope and bell. They're the same as they were the night before. He gently tugs on it to make sure the bell still works and fights off the dread he feels. Mother should have alerted him by now.

You're doing everything you can, he tells himself, but he knows it's a lie. He could have jumped in the opening when he came to his senses. He read Cherry Raven's article about the Hawthorns. They went in twice before their final expedition.

Maybe there's a part of me that doesn't want her to come home? Maybe I'm dragging my feet on purpose. Otis shakes his head, angry at himself for thinking something so terrible. Mother loves him, and she wants him to be safe. She'd approve of his caution, his prudence.

"I'll be right back, Mother," Otis says. "I need a moment. If you ring the bell, I'll hear it."

He rubs the sleep from his eyes and heads to the house. In the kitchen, he shakes four Tylenol into his palm and gulps them down with two glasses of water. Then he strips off his filthy button-down—something he should have done yesterday—and tosses it down the cellar stairs. It's probably ruined. Just another thing that's gone wrong.

Upstairs, he cleans himself in the sink, pulls on a white cotton undershirt, and debates throwing on another dress shirt to look good for Mother when she returns, but decides against it. One ruined shirt is enough.

He's combing his hair when a death shout cuts the air and chills his guts. What he's hearing is the sound of someone being murdered. And he knows who the voice belongs to—Amelia.

Checking the closest window, he confirms his fears; Amelia's Oldsmobile is parked in the driveway, in the same place it was not fifteen minutes ago. Anger wells up inside him as he jets down the stairs and outside toward the opening. He reaches the corner of the barn and skids to a stop. Amelia leans precariously against the weathered wooden structure, facing him, her weight ready to drag her to the ground any second. Violet light silhouettes her as she takes small, struggling steps toward him, or more likely, her Oldsmobile.

"What did you do?" he shouts. He ignores Amelia, rushes past her, and jerks down the drop cloths, hiding the opening again.

"You didn't see anything," he croaks, wheeling on her. He's ready to grab her by the back of her neck and shove her to her car. Storming past, he cuts in front of her. But his outrage evaporates when he realizes what's happening. Rivulets of sweat roll down her jowls, and her lips are stretched tight in a grimace. She's having a heart attack—another one. And she barely survived the first two years ago. Her eyes bulge with fear at the sight of him.

"Stay away from me," she whines. With one hand on the barn, she takes two more shuffling steps toward her car, collapses to her knees, and slams face-first into the ground.

Dropping beside her, Otis carefully rolls Amelia to her back. His ears are replete with the suck and blow of her labored breathing. Her brown eyes are unfocused and rattle back and forth. *What will Mother think when she comes back and her only friend has died in their front yard?* He won't let that happen.

"Amelia, can you hear me?"

She groans.

"What do you need? Tell me what to do?

"Pills," she slurs, and motions to her car. "Purse."

"Okay, okay. I'll help you. I promise." He beelines to the vehicle and flings open the driver's door. Amelia's red purse is in the passenger seat. He scrambles into the car and franticly shoves his hand deep into the purse. All he finds is loose change, balled-up tissues, and a bulky leather wallet. In frustration, he upturns the purse. A small brown pill bottle topples out. *There you are!*

"I have them," he shouts as he jogs back to her, the bottle raised over his head like he's won a trophy. He has, in a way. He's saved Amelia. Mother will be so very proud.

He's most of the way to her when he remembers who Amelia is—a holy roller and hateful gossip. She'll tell everyone at church about the opening. Probably say it's the work of Satan. He pictures a group of men and women in crisp white shirts and khaki pants holding hands, praying for God to close the opening and save himself and Mother from sin. That's if they don't think they opened the gateway themselves.

Then he sees Mother's mortified face. She'd say her reputation was ruined, and she wouldn't be wrong. Reputation is everything in Pulaski. It's the difference between being a valued member of the community and an outcast. It's the difference between being Regina Ferryman and Ryan Cooke, the town loon who thought he saw a three-fingered monster.

Otis's quick jog turns into a trot, then a creeping walk. He comes to a complete stop four feet away from Amelia. Her eyes are locked on the clear blue sky. Her lips are moving, but she's not speaking. He doesn't need to hear her words to know what she's saying. She's praying.

All it will take to save her is to shove a pill down her throat and call for an ambulance. She might spend a night or two in the hospital, but she'd be on her feet in a week, maybe two.

Otis glares at the pills and furrows his brow. Why did she have to be such a gossip? Why did she have to peek at the opening? He had a plan. Save Mother and then reveal the opening when the time is right. He can't risk Mother's reputation or Amelia alerting the world too soon.

He kneels next to the dying woman and takes her hand.

"My pills," she gasps.

He doesn't respond immediately. Instead, he focuses on the opening. He can feel its violet light strengthen him. "I can't."

The woman shakes her head in disbelief and tries to pull her hand away, but he squeezes tighter. "Please," she says.

"It'll be okay. I'm here with you."

After twenty minutes, she stops breathing. He sits with her as the sun passes its zenith. He sits so long his skin starts to burn. Amelia bought him a blue and yellow toy truck for his fifth birthday. He loved that truck. He used to call her Aunt Amelia.

"I'm sorry."

A blowfly brings Otis back. It lands on Amelia's cheek, and he swats it away. Amelia prided herself on her cleanliness; she'd never let such a foul creature touch her skin for more than a second.

It's been hours since her death, and he's still at her side, their fingers entwined. He's been lost in anger and shock. She didn't have to die. Not if she'd minded her own business. Amelia's death was her fault, her choice. She should have gone home and waited for Mother to call her. Showed a little patience.

He peels his fingers free from her grip and rises to his feet on shaky legs. His entire body aches with every movement. Staring down at Amelia's body, he tells himself he's not a murderer. He can't be; Mother raised him better. Not giving Amelia her pills isn't the same as plunging a hunting knife into her heart or squeezing her throat until she turns purple.

Push it all away, he thinks. Mother will be back soon, and Amelia's body can't be here. Mother will be distraught when she learns her best friend died while she was away. She'll cry—real tears, not the fake ones she sometimes uses to twist his heart. He'll protect Mother from this. Later, when she's recovered from her ordeal, he'll tell her what happened to Amelia. She had a heart attack, just like thousands of people do each day. It's really not that abnormal, and besides, look at Amelia; she never took care of herself, not like she should have.

No, Amelia's body can't stay. The easiest thing to do, the simplest, most direct thing, would be to throw the body into the opening. But he can't do that. Mother might see. He has to make her death look natural. He must take Amelia home. Make her someone else's problem.

His arms and hands are slick with sweat, so he wipes them across the front of his white shirt, staining it. *Another shirt ruined*, he thinks, and fights hard not to smack Amelia's corpse. He'll need to change again. Mother likes clean boys.

Now that his skin is dry, he squats behind Amelia's head, slides his arms deep under her armpits, and pulls. Something pops, and sharp pain knifes his lower back.

"Argh!" He drops Amelia, and her head thumps off the grass. "You deserve what happened to you," he hisses.

When the pain subsides, he tries again. He drags her five feet at a time then rests, bent over, hands on knees, lungs desperate for air. It goes on like this until he reaches Amelia's gaudy Oldsmobile and manhandles her body into the backseat. He slams the door in frustration and collapses against the side of the vehicle, exhausted and pissed off. He catches the scent of sour vinegar rolling off his body and his stomach knots. *Gross*, he thinks. *No more alcohol. Not for me, not for Mother. Sober until the Apocalypse.*

When he's nearly caught his breath, he looks back at the opening. One of Amelia's soft black shoes is out in the grass. It sticks out like a black eye on a pale, unblemished face. He wants to scream at the shoe. If he could start fires with his mind, he'd burn it up. Just once today, he wishes something would go right. Holding his lower back, he limps to the shoe and snatches it up. He throws it at the Oldsmobile in anger, but he's tired and sore, and the shoe dives straight into the ground. Picking up the shoe a second time, he squeezes it as hard as he can, but he's not strong enough to crush it. He accomplishes nothing more than bending it a little. *Fine*, he thinks and drops it into the vehicle.

He parts his hair with his fingers and shuffles to the opening. "Mother, I need to run an errand. I'll be back soon."

Everything in his body tells him he shouldn't leave. Because if he leaves, Mother will pull the rope and ring the bell. And if he's not there to pull her out, she'll never ring the bell again.

He tells himself not to think like that. He can't think like that. Mother is coming home.

The Oldsmobile's keys are in the ignition. He settles in and adjusts the seat and mirror before turning the engine over. A powerful man's voice crackles through the speakers. It belongs to a local preacher whose church broadcasts sermons throughout the week. "Without your elders, you who are in your youth will lose your connection to God," the man says.

He turns in his seat to speak to Amelia's corpse. She lays on her side, facing him, one arm pinned under her bulk, the other draped across her head. "You would have loved this sermon," he says, but one look at her empty eyes dries the hate on his tongue. "Sorry," he adds, quickly twisting around to adjust the radio dial. He flips through the stations until the bouncy beat of "Papa-Oom-Mow-Mow" bops through the car. It's a nonsense song, he knows, but it always makes Mother smile.

Sixteen minutes later, Otis wheels the Oldsmobile into Amelia's driveway. Her house is short and stately, with a stern picket fence. He parks in the garage and closes the door, sealing himself in darkness. Only then does he relax. He passed one car on the way to Amelia's and it had an out-of-state license plate. There's no way the driver would know Amelia King wasn't behind the wheel of her own car. He counts himself lucky for that. In a small town, everyone knows everything about everybody. It wouldn't be completely strange that he was driving Amelia's car, but it'd be memorable.

He steps out of the vehicle and feels around until he finds the light switch. He flips it and a muted yellow light fills the garage. *Do this quick and get out*, he tells himself. *You need to be there when Mother rings the bell. She's counting on you.*

He opens the door to the back seat and wraps his small hands around Amelia's thick calves. Surprisingly, her skin is smooth and supple. There's not a hair to be found. Ignoring the pain in his back, he tugs at the corpse. Amelia's body rustles across the backseat upholstery before slowly sliding onto the cement floor. It'd be easier to pull Amelia's body inside using her knees, but he refuses to do so. He can't explain why—it's simply undignified. He can do that much for Amelia, at least. He can treat her body with respect. Some respect, anyway.

Like before, moving Amelia's corpse is a slow, excruciating process. He hauls her through the garage door into the kitchen, then adjusts her body and begins the second leg of the journey. Her flesh squeals across the tile floor as he drags her toward the living room, making him wince.

The living room is spotless, and every flat surface is lined with porcelain figurines, each the size of Otis's thumb. Seeing them makes him feel like he's in the world's saddest museum. An ancient box TV is pressed against the far wall. Across from it is a floral couch with a heavy dip on the left side where Amelia must have sat to watch her shows, the same ones Mother watches. If Otis had a dollar for every time he heard the two of them talk about their soaps, he wouldn't need to sell the opening—he'd already be rich.

Stepping back from the corpse, he scans the room, unsure where to place it. His first thought is to prop her on the sofa and call it a day. She was going to die there eventually. It's not much of a lie if he makes it look like she actually did. But his guts say the sofa isn't right. Amelia was a stubborn woman; she would have taken her impending death seriously. She would have fought for her pills.

He carries Amelia's body closer to the kitchen and adjusts it so it looks like she collapsed and fell while attempting to find her pills. He's thankful he remembered to bring those.

The pills rattle as he pulls them out of his pocket. *A death rattle*, he thinks, with a morbid touch of humor. He sets them on the kitchen counter near the sink and contemplates his decision. The bottle doesn't look right in the space, so he heads back to the car and repacks Amelia's purse, making sure to bury her medication at the bottom. He drops the bag on the counter and feels good about the decision. Next, he plucks grass from Amelia's hair and dress.

He's sure he thought of everything, but now he's uncertain of how to proceed. He looms over the body. This is her final goodbye. He should say something. She made him want to pull his hair out by the handful, but she could sometimes be nice. "Mother will miss you. We'll visit your grave often. I know you'd like that."

Back in the garage, he pulls Amelia's shoes from the back seat and places them inside the house next to several other pairs. Finally, it's time to leave. He opens the automatic door. Halfway up, one of Amelia's neighbors rolls past the house in their black sedan. His stomach sinks, and in a panic, he drops the car keys and jabs the garage door button, freezing the panels in place. *Close call*, he thinks, while bending over to fetch the keys.

As he touches them, an uncomfortable realization flashes through his mind. He thought he was so clever, taking Amelia's body back to her house. Not once did he consider how he was going to get back to Mother. Such a stupid, stupid boy.

"Shit," he says. He'll have to walk back. And he can't do that in the daylight and not be seen. His only choice is to wait until dark.

Mother is going to be so mad at me.

Otis waits two hours after sunset to start his journey. He sneaks out of Amelia's backdoor and creeps out of her neighborhood to Orchard Way, the winding two-lane road he must travel to get back to Mother. Stepping onto the asphalt does nothing to lower his anxiety. He's been gone for too long already, and now, by his estimate, he has an hour-and-a-half walk in front of him. *Why didn't I hide Amelia in the barn and deal with her later?* he asks himself before breaking into a fast walk along the shoulder.

Over the years, Otis has driven Orchard more times than he can remember and never thought much about it. It's simply the fastest way to get to Amelia's house and most places in Pulaski. In the silvery moonlight and on foot, though, the road is different altogether. It stretches out before him, winding and bending and hugging the terrain. Trash litters its shoulder, the drainage ditch beside it, and the spikey underbrush beyond that. Worse, without a car, he feels exposed. If he's not careful, he could end up roadkill for vultures.

Twenty minutes into the walk, a car emerges from the distant darkness, rumbling toward him, its headlights growing brighter with each heartbeat. Terrified of being spotted, he flings himself off the shoulder over the ditch and into the underbrush. Jagged sticks jab and prick at him as if to punish him for his transgressions. He presses himself flat to the ground next to a Mountain Dew bottle that smells of chewing tobacco. The foul stench overwhelms his nostrils, and he gags. Seconds later, the car barrels past.

Wincing from the pain in his back, he shuffles to his feet, smacks at a mosquito harassing his ear, and starts again. He barely makes it fifty feet before he hears another car, this time from behind. He contemplates squatting instead of hiding but decides against it.

Again, he dives off the shoulder. He slides down the muddy drainage ditch and lands in inch-deep standing water. His stomach wrenches on impact, and he bites back a curse. The rotten torso of a dead possum lies at the top of the ditch, eye level with him. It takes all his resolve to wait until the vehicle's tail lights disappear into the night before he scrambles out of the ditch. *Why the hell are there so many people out tonight?*

Socks squishing inside his shoes, he presses on. He makes it a reasonable distance this time before another vehicle—a white, egg-shaped van that he's certain belongs to Mr. O'Brien, the county clerk—appears out of the moonlit darkness headed toward his home. It'd be so simple to wave the man down, catch a ride, and end this dreadful march. A lie is already forming on his tongue. His truck broke down a while back, and with it being dark out, anyone could miss it. And the mud? That's simple: he slipped. Clumsy, clumsy, clumsy.

But he knows he shouldn't. He's come this far; he can go a little farther and be brave and strong for Mother. Disappointed in himself for even considering flagging Mr. O'Brien down, he sneaks into the underbrush again and waits until the van passes before he starts his walk once more.

So the night goes. He trundles forward one foot after the other, and time becomes meaningless. The cars keep coming, the trucks keep coming, the motorcycles keep coming. And each time he hears their engines, he hides on the side of the road, with the trash and mud and festering roadkill.

The wail of an ambulance in the distance snaps his funk. Someone out there is hurt. Or dying. Just like Mother. He breaks into a pathetic jog. Little bursts of determination carry him for thirty seconds, sometimes forty, before he's forced to walk again, hands on his side.

Dawn is still hours away when he reaches his driveway. The cold night air has seeped into his flesh, and he's on the verge of shivering uncontrollably. His mouth is dry and tacky, and if he were to listen hard, he knows he would hear his bones grind inside the desiccated husk that is his body. *All this for Mother.*

What Otis wants is to limp to the house, drink a gallon of iced tea, and gnaw on a fatty piece of meat. He wants to scrub Amelia's odor off his flesh, pick the trash out of his hair, and sleep until noon.

Not yet, he tells himself as he limps up the driveway toward the shed. *Mother is waiting for me.*

Everything is the same as he left it. The opening's violet light leaks from the shed. Mother's handbell is still quiet. He pulls back the cloths covering the opening and watches it undulate hypnotically.

"I'm back, Mother," he says. "If you're there, pull the rope. All you have to do is pull the rope, and I'll bring you home. Pull the rope for your baby boy."

He drops to his knees as worry grips his being. Mother should have pulled the rope and rang her bell by now. A thought he's tried hard to repress creeps forward, demanding his attention. *What if Mother's gone? What if she's never coming home?*

He doesn't want this thought. It stings his soul. "No, no, no," he murmurs with a heavy tongue. "You're not naughty. You're a good boy." He punctuates the sentence by pounding his palm into the side of his head.

When he's had enough, he lumbers to his feet. He knows what he must do to bring Mother home. "If you won't come to me, I'll come to you," he says to the opening. "I should have done it already. That's what you're waiting for, isn't it?"

He shuffles to the opening and stops, inches before it. The smell of sweet honey and death attacks his senses. One more step and he'll be inside the opening with Mother. He'll take her gently into his arms and carry her to safety.

"I'm coming," he says, not for Mother but himself. If he says the words enough times, maybe he'll believe them.

Seconds turn to minutes. He wants to leap inside the opening but can't bring himself to do it. All he can think about are John and Kat Hawthorn and how they never came home. "I can't do this," he eventually says, shame slumping his shoulders. "I'm so, so sorry."

Instead of retreating, he rubs his cheek with his knuckles and stares into the pulsing light, hoping for a sign, hoping Mother is strong enough to save herself.

A shadow ripples across the center of the opening so fast that he isn't sure if it's real or his imagination. It doesn't matter, though. The thought of Mother inches away from him jackrabbits his heart with joy.

There it is again!

A cylindrical object the diameter of a wine bottle tears through the opening's membrane. Ribbons of thick, white ooze roll off it, forming a quivering puddle at his feet. Frozen in anticipation, he waits, his right hand glued to his cheek, the hair on his arms and the back of his neck ridged.

The viscous discharge drips and slides off the object for so long that he thinks it might never stop. The world will drown in it. God's new reset button. But it does stop flowing, and as the last of the stomach-churning goo falls away, he gasps. A slender hand, a woman's hand, waits patiently for him.

Mother has come home! The realization jolts him into action. He grabs Mother's hand to pull her out, and as he does, she clutches his wrist so tight her nails bite into his flesh, mixing his frightened blood into the ooze. Hissing the pain away, he tugs at Mother's arm, but he can't break her free, so he pulls harder using both hands. "Come out!" he cries into the night. "What's wrong with you?"

Then she starts to pull him toward the opening, and he goes stiff with shock. How is she so strong? "Let me go! I don't want to go inside!" He beats at her terrible hand, but it doesn't matter. Screaming as loud as he can, he summons everything he hates about Mother: her arrogance, her spite, her manipulations, and yanks his arm from her unnatural grasp.

Pinwheeling, he falls backward and bangs his head on the ground. Explosions of bright light burst across his vision, and his lungs refuse to work.

When he can breathe again, he sits up and searches for Mother's hand. It's gone. *She's gone. What have I done?* A high-pitched wail rises from deep in his belly and bursts from his throat. It goes on and on until he doesn't have the strength to continue and collapses back to the ground. He closes his eyes for what feels like the first time in weeks.

A sharp, familiar sound jolts him upright—Mother's bell is ringing. Beside him, the nylon rope whips up and down chaotically, rattling the handbell so hard that his back teeth want to explode. *Mother wants to be pulled out!*

"Hold on tight! Be strong for your baby boy!"

He's behind the wheel of his pickup truck in seconds. Through the rearview mirror, he eyes the opening and fights the urge to gun the gas pedal. Instead, he presses it gently, lovingly.

Slick rope slides from the opening, splattering goo over the ground until, at last, the back of Mother's wheelchair breaks through the membrane. "Aah!" he screams and taps the gas one more time to end his nightmare.

Then his joy sours, and his chest tightens so fast that he chokes. The wheelchair is empty. *Where is she?*

He totters to the wheelchair and glares at it, his body numb. He doesn't know how—not yet—but he's certain it's the wheelchair's fault that Mother isn't with him now. "You piece of shit!" he barks, before knocking the wheelchair over and stomping on the spokes again and again.

When he's had his fill, he turns his attention to the opening. "I have to do it, don't I? That's the only way." He launches the wheelchair aside and confronts the opening again. His right hand quivers as he plunges it into the opening. It's like sticking his hand into warm snot. Choking down vomit, he probes farther.

Something soft caresses his palm, and he pulls away, leaving most of his arm inside the entity. Every instinct inside him tells him to run.

"Take my hand!" he calls out, ignoring his lizard brain, and again drives his arm deep into the opening. Another caress waits for him, this time against the tender flesh of his inner forearm. He doesn't wait for Mother to take his hand. He snatches her wrist and pulls with all his will. Freeing her is like dragging an anchor through a pond filled with Vaseline. With one final burst of strength, he rips her from the opening and staggers backward, where he collapses.

Mother lays naked and unmoving, lathered in mucus, her features obscured by the creamy goo. Haloed in the opening's strange light, he thinks this must be what an angel looks like. Tears of relief stream from his cheeks. He hurries to Mother's side and drags her into his lap. Delicately, he begins to wipe the discharge from her face. "It's okay," he says. "I'm here, Moth—"

A young woman with raven black hair and piercing blue eyes stares up at him.

"Who are you?"

"It's me, baby boy."

Mother leans on Otis as he guides her to the downstairs bathroom. He leaves her to clean herself and, unsure what to do next, wanders the house in a stupor, shuffling from the kitchen to the living room to the dining room and back. The pipe rattle and hiss of Mother's shower brings him back to the present. Like Mother, he's covered in the sickly-sweet discharge, only for him, it's just the top layer of grime covering his skin. At the kitchen sink, he dampens a handful of dish towels and sloughs off mud, sweat, and ooze from his body.

"Is this really happening?" he asks himself as he finishes. Mother is young again. Younger than he is. She looks exactly like she does in her beauty pageant photos hanging in the dining room. It should be impossible, but dimensional tears should also be impossible.

A dark, cold thought squeezes his heart and loosens his bowels. *Mother is going to be alive for a long, long time now.* Fear setting in, he starts to pace again and finds himself back in the dining room surveying the remnants of Mother's special meal. He can't go on like this anymore. Things must change, or one of them will do something they can never take back.

I'll do something I can never take back.

He must get out. He needs her to understand. He should have done it long ago, before he discovered the opening.

Hurriedly, he shoves the remainder of last night's meal into an extra-large garbage bag and tosses it out the backdoor. The one thing he keeps is the cake he baked for her. He places it on the table along with new plates and silverware.

Afterward, he fetches Mother's handbell and sets it in front of her chair at the head of the table. He still hates it, yet it's somehow fitting Mother should have it, even if she doesn't need it anymore. She's used it for so long that it's an extension of her body.

A soft creak from across the room frightens him, and he spins toward it. Mother is in the doorway between the kitchen and dining room. No longer covered in the ooze, she looks even younger than he first thought. Her dark hair hangs in waves to her shoulders. A deep blue dress with copper buttons accentuates her slim waist.

"Come in, sit," he says as he pulls Mother's seat back for her. "Are you hungry?"

"Very," she says, taking her place at the table.

Hands shaking, he slices a piece of cake, plates it, and slides it across the table. Mother gives him a toothy smile, and without so much as a thank-you, devours the confection in three ravenous bites.

"What happened to you?" he asks.

Instead of answering, Mother cuts herself another piece of cake, larger than the first, and inhales it just as fast. When finished, she rolls a probing gaze at him. He can't meet her disappointed eyes and studies the table instead. He needs a drink, never mind that he swore off booze less than twelve hours ago. "I'm— I'm sorry," he says when the silence becomes too much for him to bear.

Mother's hand slides across the table and grasps his. "I thought I raised you better."

"You did. It's not your fault. It's mine."

"At least, there's something we can both agree on. It's always your fault."

Otis's lungs catch. A jumble of emotions threatens to tear him apart; he hates and loves Mother equally. He wants nothing and everything to do with her.

"I'm going to make it up to you," he says. He inhales deeply and sighs. "Mother, I'm going to move out. I have to. I can sell the rights to the opening—I mean, that gateway to wherever you were. There's money in it."

Mother pats his hand. "I want you to go to your room and think about what you've done to me… And Amelia."

Otis feels the blood drain from his face. "You saw me?" he asks more forcefully than he intended. "It was an accident!"

"Go to your room, baby boy. I'll ring for you when you can come down."

"I'm an adult. You can't ground me."

"And you're not leaving."

He jerks his hand away. "I have to. Look at what this place made me do."

Mother shakes her head as if in disbelief. "I'd like a rum and Coke."

"You're not listening."

"I am listening, but I want to listen with a rum and Coke. Please."

The world feels almost normal again. "Yes, Mother. Of course."

In the kitchen, he opens the refrigerator and bends down to pull a can from the case at the bottom of the shelf. As he reaches in, he hears Mother's footsteps behind him. "I can do it myself," he says.

He pulls the can from the fridge and turns to her. She's clutching her handbell so tight her knuckles are white. "Why do you have—"

Mother lashes out with the bell, smashing it into his temple. He stumbles back from the force of the strike and crashes into the open refrigerator. Food rains down on him. The last thing he sees before everything goes dark is blood dripping off the bell.

The duct tape is tight against Otis's chest. His wrists are immobile. His ankles fettered. He's strapped to Mother's slime-covered wheelchair and parked in front of the undulating opening. Warm urine fills his lap. "Don't do this!"

Mother is behind him. He can sense her presence. "I know you're scared, baby boy. But I need you to be brave for Mother. You know I like it when you're brave." Her tone is patronizing, the speech of an adult speaking to a five-year-old who's about to be pricked by a needle.

"I won't go," he shouts and rocks back and forth to tip himself over.

"Don't," she says, "or I'll have to hit you again."

He ignores her and rocks harder. The right wheel hovers off the ground for the briefest moment. He coils for another attempt, but before he can throw his weight to the side, Mother appears beside him and drives her bell into his hands so hard he feels his fingers snap.

"I warned you," she says and disappears behind him again. She pushes him toward the opening.

"What's inside?" Otis pleads, tears rolling down his cheeks. "Tell me!"

"I raised you wrong. I spoiled you. Let you do whatever you wanted. I won't make that mistake again."

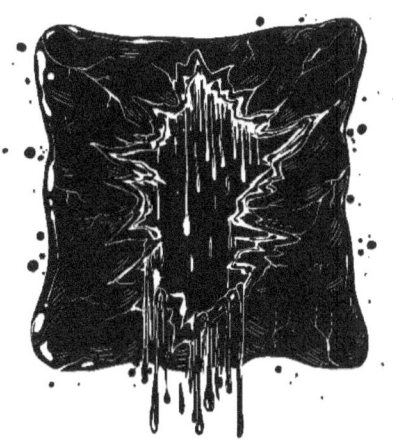

COME TO DADDY
Ryan T. Jenkins

The Lord said to Satan, "Where have you come from?" Satan answered the Lord, "From roaming throughout the earth, going back and forth on it."

—Job 1:7

There's nothing more punk rock than being a dad.
   —T-shirt worn by an anonymous dad at a punk show

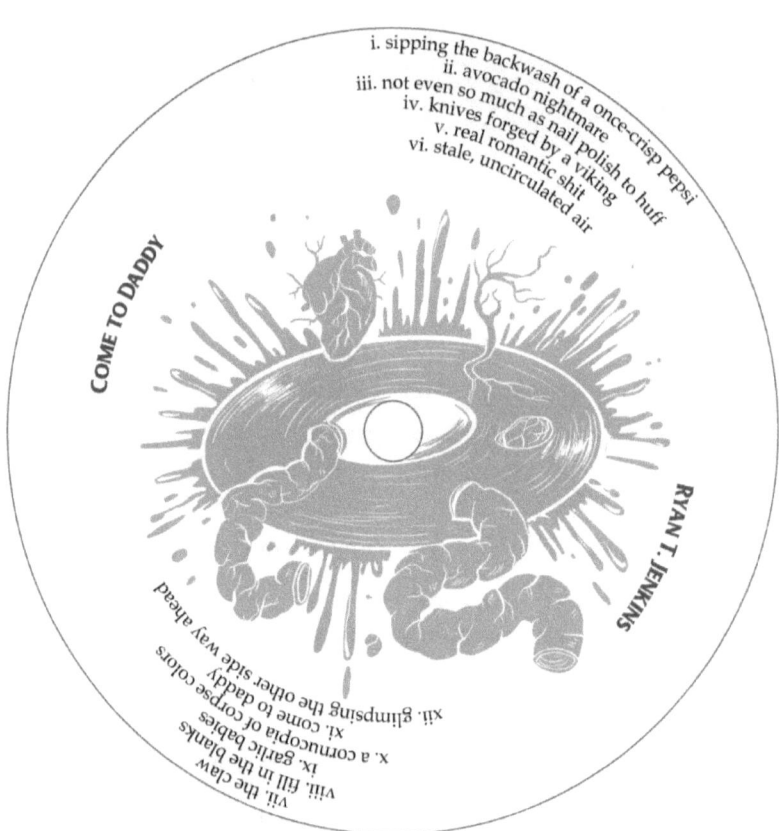

COME TO DADDY

RYAN T. JENKINS

i. sipping the backwash of a once-crisp pepsi
ii. avocado nightmare
iii. not even so much as nail polish to huff
iv. knives forged by a viking
v. real romantic shit
vi. stale, uncirculated air
vii. the claw
viii. fill in the blanks
ix. Garlic babies
x. a cornucopia of corpse colors
xi. come to daddy
xii. glimpsing the other side way ahead

i.
sipping the backwash of a once-crisp pepsi

Today is moving day into my new house, and I'm frothing with the same excitement I used to get just before stepping into a punk show in my twenties. It's like I'm standing outside the venue now, a recently minted divorcé at forty-four years old, and can hear all the drunk roadies doing the sound check inside, striking the guitars, the squeals of feedback, the *boom boom boom* of the bass drums vibrating in my gut, the impatient rumblings of the crowd. It's never too late to start again on life.

Or at least that's what Dr. Singh writes in the introduction of his book, *Mid-Lifers: Become a Superhero and Conquer Your Middle-Life Crisis*:

"Old dogs learn new tricks all the time. You can be that old dog."

Gearing up for the move, I pop a couple Addies, wash my face in a motel bathroom that might as well be a cockroach farm, pack up my shit, and do one final sweep of the room to ensure I'm not, God forbid, leaving any chargers behind. Then my cell rings. It's the moving company. I answer it. Dmitri, the head moving consultant, prattles on incoherently.

"Say that again," I say.

Dmitri speaks slower, as if I were a child. "Your . . . stuff . . . was taken off the truck . . . into storage. Once in storage . . . your items . . . got all jumbled up . . . with other people's stuff . . . by mistake."

"How does this happen?" I ask, pacing the motel room I've been living in for the past two weeks, ready more than ever to get out of this drab hellscape, with its blaring beige and screaming gray décor and offensive lack of cheesy art.

"We don't know, sir. Prank possibly?"

"A prank? So, when am I getting my stuff back?"

"We mail things as we find them."

"How will you know what's my stuff?"

"We have things labeled. We will figure it out."

I'm literally scratching my head now. None of it is adding up.

"Sir?" Dimitri cuts in.

"Yeah."

"I bring you what I have now in the truck. I knock off five percent from the bill. We apologize for any inconvenience. And thank you for choosing Buttery Smooth Moving Services."

An hour later, I pull up to my new house, and my mood lifts. Seeing the new humble abode gives me hope—granted, it's shit-encrusted hope, like sipping the backwash of a once-crisp Pepsi—but still, something tells me that maybe I can salvage what's left of my life. Jumpstart a new routine. Meditate daily. Cut back on weed and pills and booze and ultra-processed sugars. Eat leafier greens. Read the daily newspaper, an actual newspaper, not the garbage flying around on the socials. Take up woodworking and gardening. Do yoga. Recycle my beer cans. When you've been married to somebody for eighteen-odd years, it's a bit difficult to imagine what it will look like without them, so filling in the gaps of my future has become my most recent obsession.

Which is exactly what I'm doing as I stand before 302 Crooked Way, gazing at my quaint fixer-upper that's lined with woods on either side. Plenty of privacy but still close enough to the elderly woman next door that I'm able to leech off her Wi-Fi.

I mount the front stairs slowly, like I'm a trespasser, not really sure if this heap of wood is actually mine. A sunken-in portion of the porch reminds me the house needs a shit ton of work, the only reason somebody like me could afford a house to begin with. The foundation has a major structural crack, causing it to lean slightly to the left. A few windows are missing glass. The pipes apparently need to be replaced unless I want to risk lead poisoning. The water heater and HVAC are busted. And there's the usual interior cosmetics. Missing doors, warped floorboards, cracked mirrors, termite damage. A sizable hole in the master bedroom's ceiling where a fan used to be.

I hear the rumble of an engine and turn to see a moving truck, with a faded yellow stick of butter decal painted on the side, arrive. Dmitri jumps out with a big fake smile.

"Hello, there! Beautiful day, wouldn't you say?"

"Uh-huh. Just like a U2 song," I say under my breath.

Dmitri and a big-boned mover—gnawing on a chicken biscuit—walk to the rear of the truck. Dmitri lifts the roll-up door and instead of brimming with my junk, the truck is empty, except for two cardboard boxes and an old mildew-ridden love seat that Darla and I used to store in the basement.

"This is it?" I say.

Dmitri smiles again and pats my back. "Not to worry. We find your stuff. We mail it to you the moment we find it."

I don't speak, because I don't know what to say. So, I stand there like a garden gnome and watch as Dmitri and Chicken Biscuit take five minutes to unload my measly possessions. Then they are gone.

I go into the house and find it exceedingly quiet. When I toured it at the open house, the Realtor had been blasting Coltrane so loud, I could barely think. But now, without the Coltrane, the house holds a catacomb-injected silence.

Three bedrooms. One barely functioning bath and one decent half bath. Two stories. Not bad for a single man. I already know what I'm going to do with the layout. One room will be the master bedroom. Another will be a guest room if my son, Thom, wants to visit (wishful thinking), and the final room will be my home office, since I work from home as a data inputter for a data management company called SXTL Data Management Incorporated.

I float from room to room, imagining the end product for each room's design. I retrieve a broom and sweep up dirt and cobwebs that the previous owners didn't take the time to clean, like most things with this place. At least they left behind a broom, I think.

When I get to the hypothetical office room, I freeze in my tracks, choking the broom handle.

The room is barren, like all the others, except for a movie poster hanging on the wall. The movie is called *Come to Daddy*, and it features a strikingly dramatic image of Elijah Wood holding a two-pronged devil's fork, his doe-like eyes bulging from his skull.

I stare at the poster for some time, unsettled by its presence. In my mind, Elijah Wood has always been typecast as a hobbit, but in this movie, whatever it is—it's certainly not a movie I ever saw or even heard of—he wears an expression halfway between terror and desperation.

I turn around and busy myself with something else.

ii.
avocado nightmare

Sleep isn't easy my first night in the house. Not because of bumps in the night, or the ghost of a headless demonic child (as badass as that would be), or the nasty mildew-ridden love seat I'm sleeping on that reeks worse than a landfill, or even that disconcerting Elijah Wood poster that makes me queasier the more I think about it. Nope, I'm losing sleep over my failed marriage. Over Darla. Over our divorce. Over how our marriage crashed and burned so suddenly all because of the avocados that I'd picked up at a grocery store.

It started on the day of Thom's high school graduation party. Darla was making an epic-sized portion of guacamole, and I was responsible for the margaritas, which entailed nothing more than pulling the blender and liquor bottles out of cabinets and then spending the rest of the morning taking tiny secret sips of tequila. Thom was due to arrive later in the day with some friends, so it was a waiting game for me.

The day crackled with tense energy between Darla and I. We hadn't slept together in months leading up to Thom's inevitable departure to college, meaning I had taken to residing on the couch most of the time. On the morning of the party, neither Darla nor I made eye contact, let alone talked to each other. Darla, I knew, was approaching the empty-nest situation with dreaded resistance. I was sad about it, too, but also happy for Thom. The kid, being smart and responsible, was going to grow wings and soar like that transparent woman on *In Utero*. Darla, on the other hand, was one sneeze away from dissolving into despair. I could tell she was near a breaking point because she was sucking on her pinky finger. Last time she did that was when she found out her dad had died.

So we gave each other a wide berth and we went about our morning routines in anally tight silence. She hung goofy generic streamers with those graduation hats from the ceiling and prepped a smorgasbord of finger food, including Thom's staples—a huge bowl of guac, homemade Bagel Bites, and banana bread. The silence was something normal for me, but for Darla, who talked often and with much regularity, it made the whole morning seem like we were getting ready for a funeral. At the very least,

Darla is usually playing some music, even if it's My Chemical Romance or AFI—gag—but not on this day.

As a final graduation celebration, Thom had gone on a camping trip with his friends the day prior, and was due to return late morning. Darla's sister was also coming with her husband. Darla was in the kitchen working frantically, and I was in our makeshift bar area, staring out the sliding glass door, getting a wee bit drunker moment by moment. Then I heard Darla say, "Oh my god," and I looked over to see her holding one of the avocados split open, its rotten brown meat exposed. She stared at it for quite some time, as a series of strange expressions scrolled across her face. When she peered up, my stomach knotted. Never had she looked so pained.

"What is wrong with you?" she said. "What the *fuck* is wrong with you?"

I had nothing to say for myself. She'd entrusted me to go to the Hispanic grocery store and pick out the perfect ripe-enough avocados to make Thom's favorite dish. And I'd failed.

She snorted, giggled, as tears tracked down her cheeks. "Not a word from you? What a surprise." Then she slammed her fist on the cutting board, causing me to nearly fall out of my barstool. "You know how hard it is to get *fucking* avocados around here," she said, pain turning to rage. "Mateo's is closed today. *Closed*. You know that." She cut open another avocado and found it to be just as rotten as the last one. Then another. Same. Fifteen rotten avocados. How I'd managed to pull off such a royally stupid mistake, I still don't know to this day. It's not like I'm some ignoramus when it comes to gauging an avocado's ripeness. Actually, if I may humble-brag, avocado hunting has always been one of the few things I've been competent at in my lifetime.

Which made the whole situation all the more offensive to Darla. She belted out a primal scream that I could imagine she would let out if she found Thom's dead body lying on a street corner. A scream sticky with pain so wrenching, it refuses to uncling from the heart's membrane.

I got up from the barstool and approached her cautiously. Before I could reach her, she picked up one of the rotten avocados and launched it at my face, and then another, and another, Tommy gun style. Since the avocados had been sliced open, the brown liquified fruit splattered all over the floor and furniture and walls. One connected with my forehead and exploded like a water balloon, the spoiled avocado drenching my cheeks and eyes. Another avocado hit me square on the mouth, the avocado pit miraculously slipping between my teeth. I fell to my knees, choking, but managed to spit the pit out onto the floor.

"Darla," I moaned. "Please stop! What's wrong?"

But the only response I got was the clicking of the front door, and her car firing up.

iii.

not even so much as nail polish to huff

A box of gardening tools arrives in the mail, with a quickly scrawled note from Dmitri.

Found these. Thank u!

I curse him under my breath. So far, over the past few weeks since moving in, I've received a squeaky ottoman, a bookcase with a broken shelf, and a couple boxes with miscellaneous household items. Still no bed. I contemplated, on several occasions, buying a new one at Walmart, but knowing my relationship with the universe, the second I bought a new bed, my old bed would arrive at the doorstep.

I shrug it off. Who in the hell is going to visit me anyway? I have no visitors. Thom isn't coming, that's clear enough. I haven't heard from him since the avocado disaster when I made his girlfriend—what's-her-face— scream like Janet Leigh. So, in the grand scheme of my midlife, furniture doesn't matter. Not a whole lot matters, really, the more I dwell on it all. Not for a pitiful soul like myself who eats peanut butter saltines for lunch and mayonnaise sandwiches for dinner and enters endless lists of numbers into spreadsheets for work (still not clear what all the numbers mean, to be honest).

The only thing that is starting to reach past my numbness at this point is Elijah Wood. Well, the poster of him in my home office. It's like my nanny's old wooden doll set that she hand-painted herself and lined up around the house. The problem was Nanny loved her happy pills and painted the dolls' mouths too large and their eyes too little, so wherever you went in the house you were always greeted by an audience of grotesque faces. Major creep vibes. Not in a good way. Not in the Misfits' album covers kind of way. More in the way that it makes me want to scratch my scalp over and over again until it bleeds.

So, due to this, I've decided to remote-work from the mildew love seat for the time being. It also doesn't hurt that it's a good solid ten feet closer to the old woman's Wi-Fi next door. When I'm getting up to pee or take a cold shower every week or so, I steal peeks at the poster through the open office door. Glances mainly. No staring. Call me crazy but I don't like to stare at Elijah Wood wielding a devil's fork. It's like having a possum in the house and not enough gall to get rid of it. As long as I keep my distance, I assume that Elijah Wood will keep his distance.

Then one day, I experience what I'd call a "perfect storm of forced sobriety"—somehow, I run out of pills, weed, and beer at the exact same moment and there are no fallback substances at my disposal, not even so much as a bottle of nail polish to huff. I call the pharmacy and they say to give them three hours to refill. So I pace around the house endlessly like Escobar's pet jackrabbit, until I glide past the home office and see the poster. My pixilated mind snaps like a dry twig and I channel all my sober rage toward it, cocking my fist back like I used to do in mosh pits when some coked-up dumbshit stepped in and started flailing, not realizing there's a flow and rhythm to moshing, *god fucking dammit*. As I draw closer to the poster, I discover it's housed in a thin, nearly transparent frame bolted to the wall. I retrieve my one good butter knife and try to insert it in between the frame and the wall, but the frame won't budge. Then I try a paint scraper, which also does not work. I'm considering taking a sledgehammer to it when the pharmacy calls to let me know that my prescription has been refilled. Two hours late, but okay . . .

I race to get my medicine, making a side trip to Walmart. By the time I get home, I feel better, more relaxed, ambitious even. Let Elijah Wood be, I tell myself. Co-existence. I'm in such good spirits that I decide I'm going to knock one of the items off my "Mid-Lifer's Superhero List" that Dr. Singh encourages in the introduction to his book:

"Come up with actionable items outside of work that keep you preoccupied on the weekends so you can vanquish time!"

One of the two items on my Mid-Lifer's Superhero List—the other being chisel an owl figurine—is planting garlic in the garden out back. Some person, I don't remember who, probably Darla, told me that you can plant a clove of garlic in soil, and, with a little water and a little sunlight, it will sprout garlic plants. Easy enough for me.

I don't have a shovel, so I use an old coffee tin instead, and plant the few bulbs of garlic I got from the Walmart run. Once I smooth the dirt back over the bulbs, a sense of accomplishment settles over me.

I'm making progress in life, I tell myself. It might be in man-baby steps, but still—I would like to believe Darla and Thom would be proud of my soon-to-be lush garlic garden.

When I head back inside to pee, and just as I'm about to step into the bathroom, the Elijah Wood poster through the doorway of the home office arrests my attention again. Because at the angle I'm standing, something strikes me that I hadn't noticed before.

Elijah Wood has an uncanny resemblance to Thom.

iv.
knives forged by a viking

Two days after Thom's botched graduation party, where avocados had become literal nightmares, Darla returned home. I hadn't done much since she'd run off, but at least I'd managed to pop a few Addies and drink the rest of the tequila and clean up the avocado crime scene before she'd gotten back. She didn't seem to notice, or care, though, when she entered and sneered at me where I was sitting on the couch. She promptly informed me that a new graduation party for Thom had been scheduled for next Saturday, the "real graduation party" she was calling it, and I most definitely was *not* invited. She also informed me that she would be filing for a divorce.

"Over avocados?" I squawked in disbelief. She turned and glared at me with fire-touched eyes that suggested she was weighing out whether murdering me and going to prison for the rest of her life might be worth it.

"Are you really that far gone?" she said, then proceeded to stuff her items into trash bags and boxes, ransacking the house. I followed her around like a skittish dog, willing myself to speak but failing to do so. Was I that far gone? That'd been the question I'd been asking myself endlessly. *Was I too dumb to see that I was a real problem for Darla?*

My soul-searching over the past two days had led me to scant conclusions: First off, I'd done nothing to warrant a divorce. At least in recent memory. Mainly I kept my mouth shut and did my job. Checks came in regularly. Sure, they always took a big hit with my meds and booze, but they were usually enough to cover groceries. I'd never cheated on Darla, at least in my waking life. I wasn't physically violent, nor emotionally abusive, at least not overtly so. Sure, our romantic life had been like a fire covered in a wet rag, but we at least were a semi-functioning nuclear family, sans the nuclear part. More gas-powered, I guess you could say. At the end of the day, the house wasn't burning, and for that I felt it was worth celebrating.

She broke my concentration when she started pulling knives out of the block on the kitchen counter. "What are you doing with those?" I asked. I didn't own much, but I knew that I owned that knife set. They had been a present from my grandpaps, who'd acquired them in Denmark many years ago, claiming they'd been forged by a Viking. That was probably a lie given their age, but I suppose some sentiment had been attached to them.

She stared me down again. "It's like you give a fuck about these knives more than me."

"Because I handwash them?" I asked sincerely. It was the only thing that came to mind.

"Yup!" she screamed back, and stabbed the butcher knife directly into the countertop, splintering the wood. She went about her business of dumping the rest of the silverware into a black trash bag, leaving me a few bits of scrap to contend with.

Not long after that, I saw through the window a moving truck pull up. A giant stick of butter floating in midair. Dmitri, who I hadn't known at the time, came bumbling in with his trademark smile, along with Chicken Biscuit, and in a matter of three to four hours, gutted the house like a swarm of termites until there was next to nothing left but a few stray items lying about. Trash and dirt mainly. Boxes of junk that not even a thrift store would take. An old TV that I'd picked up at a garage sale many years ago. Worn-out clothes with unidentifiable stains imprinted into them. The mildew love seat, along with some random, terribly assembled IKEA furniture in the basement. And of course the knife set.

A few days later, I received a call from a lawyer that "our" house—technically, Darla's house—was being sold, and I had seven days to vacate.

V.
real romantic shit

A couple more months pass at 302 Crooked Way. Sporadically, more items arrive from the moving company. Boxes mainly, one containing a broken spatula and a scratched-up frying pan that Darla claimed would give us cancer, but at least I can start making grilled cheeses. I also receive a work desk with a broken drawer, three lamps without lampshades, a dented filing cabinet that requires a crowbar to open, a vertical shoe rack that must be propped against the wall to hold steady, an assortment of bagged clothes, and most important—a Mr. Joe coffeemaker missing its pot, along with an array of deformed and misunderstood mugs.

Excited, I brew up a full pot of coffee with a bag of expired grounds, using a chipped salad bowl as the pot, and lounge on the floor in the living room. The mildewy love seat is making me nauseous these days, so I'm trying to take breaks from it. As the coffee rushes to my heart—or maybe it's the extra Addy I took to celebrate the occasion of receiving a coffeemaker—I glance at the work desk sitting in the corner. An unpleasant dread nips at me. Because, well, the work desk reminds me of my home office, which reminds me of Elijah Wood wielding a devil's fork, which reminds me of his billiard ball–sized eyes, which makes me think of how fucking hard my job is going to be with Elijah Wood staring at me all day.

I wander back there with a mug of coffee and hover near the doorway, flagellating myself with the movie poster's alluring and sickening effect. Besides Elijah Wood's now uncanny resemblance to Thom—why hadn't I seen it sooner?—I'm thinking of him again because, when he turned fourteen or so, Thom fell head over heels in love with horror movies, much to my chagrin. I hated every second of watching them. It didn't matter what kind—slashers, possessed nuns, sadistic clowns—I always white-knuckled the theater armrests, fear-eating my way through a jumbo-size popcorn (reportedly having 3,800 calories). It eventually got to the point that I used the bathroom as an excuse to leave. Mostly, though, I'd do loops around the theater and play in the arcade to avoid the movie altogether.

It dawns on me, though, that those were the only times we were all together as a family in public. At those horror movies. Because of Thom.

I sip more coffee, then tiptoe into the home office. Tiptoeing might seem like a dumb thing to do, but I feel intuitively that I shouldn't disturb Elijah Wood, unless I intend to stir a cranky dragon.

I step up real close to the poster now, and it's worse than I remember. Elijah Wood's eyes. Jesus Jennifer Christ. It's like they are coming out of the fucking wall. At what point will they pop straight out of the poster and roll onto the floor?

This close up, I also note that there is the silhouette of a man in the house in the background. *Is that Daddy?* I wonder.

I whip out my phone, snapping a photo.

Back in the living room, I text the photo to Thom and type:

Come to Daddy? Have you heard of it?????

As I wait for Thom to respond, I dig through boxes and come across the famed kitchen knife set, which sets my mind a-fluttering to Darla, then to evil avocados, then to our eighteen years of marriage disappearing like an ember drowned in a stream of piss.

I lie down in the middle of the living room, staring up at the sagging, liver-spotted ceiling. My mind starts to wander, and I think back to Darla and I's origin story.

Way back in the day, I'd see Darla at punk shows, usually alone. Something drew me to her. My dick, yeah, but something more too. A cosmic attraction, I'd like to think. Beyond the elegant way she wore her black-dyed pixie cut and whimsical tattoos, I found myself smitten by how she both contorted her face in disgust while also bobbing her head to the music. Just like me, she took pleasure in the torture of the loud, chaotic noise.

Then a more specific memory settles over me like a blanket being laid for a picnic. The night when we spoke for the first time at a Robot Cocks show, a local grindy band that sounded worse than razor blades in a blender (precisely the reason I love them). When I entered the tight, cigarette-smoke-filled venue, I spotted her immediately, toward the front, like I had the previous dozen or so times at other shows. As usual, she seemed repulsed. After the show, a daring and unexpected impulse came over me to follow her out to the parking lot, where we ended up near her beat-up Volvo covered in band bumper stickers.

"Hey," I said.

"Hey," she said, wearing that same expression she had during shows, like I was a piece of gum stuck to her Converse.

"Do you want to, uh, go to the Waffle House? I always go after shows. It's a tradition, I guess you could say." I'm surprised at my words, and how many of them there were. It's probably the most articulate and most assertive I've ever been in my life.

She narrowed her eyes. "Why are you alone?"

I looked around me, as if other people should be there. "Why are *you* alone?" I said back.

She sighed, and said, "Fine. Sure. I'll go to Waffle House. I'm hungry as fuck."

Thom was born nine months later.

And that's when we got married.

Because of Thom. Because, at the time, of "tax purposes."

I sit up from the living room floor, sip some cold coffee, and try to create a timeline of our marriage on a piece of graph paper lying nearby. Not that graph paper is necessary; I just found a stack of it in one of the few boxes delivered to my house.

I give it a hard, thirty-minute think. So. Besides the Robot Cocks show, and Thom, what else was there to our marriage?

Oh boy.

I get up, make a mayo sandwich, and eat it slowly. After a while, I retreat to my beautiful garlic garden that has sprouted exhilarating green shoots. At least I will have plenty of garlic to munch on this winter. I go back inside to the graph paper, stare at it, and then take out my phone. Still no response from Thom about the poster.

Then another memory bobs to the surface, one that I'm sure I can add to the graph paper. Darla and I's five-ish-year anniversary, when we left Thom with Darla's sister and stayed at a local campground. They had cabins to rent for ten bucks a night. We got drunk and high as fuck, and I made a bonfire that nearly burned half the county down. We laughed. We had sex. We kissed and held hands and looked at the stars. We made s'mores. Real romantic shit. Then, to top it off, we woke up to a raccoon chewing on the bed frame because I'd left the cabin door open. Perfect. Better than a Hollywood rom-com.

See? I tell myself. *There's more than just Thom.* This gets my mind jogging. I list more events: making spiked hot chocolate and watching the trees sway during Hurricane Sandy; Chris and Kylie's wedding at the rest stop where they supposedly met; that time her Volvo broke down and I went to go pick her up with the Honda, but the Honda broke down too. Memories. They are there. They exist.

So, why does it feel like digging through solid rock to unearth them?

vi.

stale, uncirculated air

One night, I smoke too much Sour Diesel and illegally download *Come to Daddy* from the Pirate Bay, which takes a considerable amount of time on the elderly lady's weak-ass Wi-Fi signal. I literally have to hold my laptop over my head like a radio antenna for five hours. But once it's downloaded, I fire the movie up, not sure what exactly I'm expecting to gain by watching it, beyond feeling freaked outta my mind.

Just as the movie starts, an ear-piercing *ding* emits from my phone—a new text from Thom.

I open it.

Can we meet tomorrow for coffee? he writes, ignoring my text above about the movie poster.

Sure!!!!! I text back, unable to contain myself, proud of using only five exclamation points and deleting the five others I originally typed out. *How about at my new house!!!???*

Maybe after. Coffee would be better.

He texts me the address to a place called Brü's Gourmet Coffeehouse over in the Museum District, and we agree to meet the next day.

I send back an emoticon of the yellow-faced man with sunglasses. Five of them.

He doesn't respond, so I set my phone down. My heart is hammering hard in my chest from the prospect of seeing Thom, like the first time speaking to Darla at the Robot Cocks show all those years ago. I don't want a horror movie to ruin my good vibes, so I shut it off, saving it for another night.

The next day, I'm up and Adam before ten a.m. The day has barely started, and miracles quickly occur, i.e., I take a freezing-cold shower, splash on some cologne that I found—Thom's maybe?—in the bottom of one of the moving boxes, brush my teeth, even floss with some loose thread, and dig through more boxes until I find a suitable outfit. Not until I have put it on and look at myself in the cracked bathroom mirror do I realize, it's the same freaking outfit I was wearing at the Robot Cocks show when I first met Darla. Saggy wide-legged jeans and a Gingivitis Heart tee showing a bloodred line down the middle that says *Slit Me Open*, a reference to one of their songs.

Whatever. I'm sure Thom doesn't know it's the same outfit, so I go with it and head to the car.

I start up the Honda with a Phillips screwdriver and make my way to Brü's, a pretentious coffee joint wedged in a high-end strip mall. I consider stopping by Lowe's to get Thom a houseplant or some shit—to be fatherly and all that—but instead opt for the Shell gas station off Sycamore Ave, which I know has a huge bin of $2 DVDs. I scavenge the bin until I find a couple horror movies—*Leprechaun 4: In Space* and *Jack Frost*—then buy fifteen dollars' worth of gas and a thirty-two-ounce bottle of Bud Light for later. I'm hoping Thom will come over, and we can share it.

I'm pleased with myself for getting to the coffee joint three minutes early, but then see Thom has already arrived, and is sipping some kind of frothy drink from one of those bougie tiny coffee cups. I wave at him, and he nods his head at me. I order four muffins of various flavors, thinking that Thom and I can sample each one. I also get myself a large coffee. All told, it cost thirty-nine dollars, an amount that would give me a brain aneurysm normally, but I grin at the manbunned barista and hand over forty dollars, telling him to keep the change.

"Thom, my man," I say as I sit down with my bundle of muffins and coffee. "How you been?"

"Doing well," he says, all professional, as if he were my insurance agent.

"First year of college, how's it goin'? I know there's the freshman fifteen, but from what I remember, it's more like the freshman fifty," I say, even if I technically went to a community college, and only for one semester before dropping out.

"Busy," he responds. "Losing weight, actually."

"Good for you. So, did you get my picture? The poster in my house? *Come to Daddy.*"

"I did."

"You won't believe this. The thing was just there in the house when I bought it. It's crazy as—"

He holds up his hand like he's stopping traffic. "Sorry, but I have a study group in, like, thirty minutes, so I don't have a lot of time. I need to talk to you about something real quick." He squints his baby-blue eyes, a trait inherited from Darla considering my eyes are blacker and more shriveled-up than mouse turds. I know this squinty look from Thom. It's not good. It's the same look he gives me when I try to strike up conversations with his girlfriends.

"Hey, before you start," I cut in, "I got a sampler of muffins here. This one's, uh, I think it's squash, and then this purply-looking one is eggplant, and—"

"Stop please. Could you listen for a second?" His words lacerate me like the blades of Grandpaps's Viking knives. "I don't have time to talk about muffins. I need to . . . get this out."

"Okay," I say, and sink my teeth into the funky red-looking muffin. It's delicious, despite it being a seven-dollar muffin stuffed with vegetables.

"I had a long conversation with Mom—" he starts, then stops. He swallows once, then twice. He sips from his tiny cup. Then says, almost in a whisper, "I'm revoking your privileges to be my father. It was a hard decision, but it's one I have given a great deal of thought to."

I take a sip of my coffee, which singes my tongue. The pain is welcoming and I sip some more, then chuckle. "Revoke what now? What you talkin' 'bout, dude?"

"I had a lawyer help me with the process. In the state of Virginia . . . it's a new law . . . called adult emancipation, which allows me to legally recognize that we are not related."

"Wait a second. Like a divorce?"

He emits a perfect Thom sigh. Ever since he turned twelve, his dramatic sigh has been transmuting into an artform all its own, and now here in this coffeehouse it's a goddamn masterpiece.

"Think of it more like a symbolic gesture. It means by the state of Virginia, you are not allowed to recognize me as your son."

"Nah, that can't be real," I say. "Where did you read this? You can't divorce from your parents."

"I think it makes perfect sense to me," Thom said, his cheeks turning red. "Just because you stuck your dick in Mom does not mean we have to interact, or relate, or associate, or anything like that."

"Well, technically it does."

"Not anymore. Not by law."

"Send me the link," I say. "I need to read more—"

"I'm not your administrative assistant. Google it yourself. And as I'm politely stating now, I would much appreciate it if you would respect my emancipation wishes."

"What's the problem here? What is it I have done?"

He raises his hand again to stop me. I think if he does that one more time, I might need to slap it away.

"You seriously don't know?" Thom speaks in a louder volume. The manbunned barista side-eyes us as he munches on a carrot.

"What? No. It's why I'm asking," I say.

"You don't have one single inkling on why this conversation might be happening?"

I scarf the rest of the muffin down. "Sor-ry. No idea," I say as crumbs spill from my mouth.

"You're going to make me say it?"

"Say what?"

"Unbelievable."

"I'm here for you, my man. You know that."

His red flushes even redder. I've never seen him such a shade of crimson.

"You are a shitty father," he snaps at me. "Or you *were* a shitty father, once this paperwork goes through."

I try to focus on what he is saying, but all that's in my head is a treasure trove of Thom memories raining down through my consciousness and forming tiny little puddles. Thousands of memories filling endless amounts of graph paper.

He puts his hands over his face and talks through his fingers. "I can't believe I have to explain this. You weren't there for us, okay? Like there, there. You're not, like, evil in the traditional sense. Not like Grandpaps. You didn't abuse me or anything, you didn't even yell . . . and that's the point. You did absolutely nothing, not a goddamn thing. You're a junkie. You get high and shrink into the corner like stale, uncirculated air."

My chin vibrates slightly. I'm about to say something eloquent. I know it's there, resting at the tip of my tongue, but nothing comes out except, "How does stale, uncirculated air shrink?"

"*Listen,* Dad— I have a lot to think about," Thom says. "I'm sure you do, too, but it would be nice if . . . you know . . . you signed the paperwork, and Mom's paperwork too. Please respect our wishes. Do the right thing and leave us alone."

And then Thom gets up and rushes out of the coffeehouse, and I find myself sitting in this imitation café, devouring a now-tasteless green muffin that I then see on the menu board is avocado-pea flavor. I spit it out onto a napkin and shakily retrieve my tin can of Altoids full of pills and pop a couple.

I try to rationalize this situation, but there's a rubber-band ball in my head. One thought that doesn't fit with this thought, and another thought that doesn't fit with that thought . . .

It's not until the manbunned barista tells me that they have a two-hour limit on tables that I snap out of my reverie.

vii.
the claw

Whenever Grandpaps got upset about something, usually while brown-bagging a bottle of malt liquor, he used to say: *That old vinyl record in my head is spinning too fast again.*

After my coffee date with Thom, this is where I'm at. Restless as fuck. The record in my head spinning so chaotically, it's gonna fly off the turntable at any moment.

If I'm not lying on the living room floor like a dirt clump, which is most of the time, I'm popping Addies to get myself moving around for at least a few hours. During these "active" hours, I piddle, fidget, unpack more boxes, hang up a coatrack missing two hooks that came the prior week, separate a cardboard box of random screws into piles of varying sizes, pace, slap myself across the face in front of the cracked bathroom mirror and watch what my cheeks look like when I do it, pace more, blast music from my youth through shitty headphones until there's nothing but a braying blur of sound, pace even more, and sometimes while pacing, glare at the closed door of my home office.

I use up all my personal and vacation days for the next two weeks, receiving a nasty email from my manager, but I don't care. *Fire me,* I think. *I dare you. I input numbers into a fucking spreadsheet forty hours a fucking week. I will just find another fucking spreadsheet job with another fucking spreadsheet company.*

I write back: *I am very sorry for the inconvenience. Namaste!*

Night is worse than daytime. At least during the daytime, I can catch a wink. At night, sleep is elusive and thorny. This becomes doubly so when a recurring childhood dream—which I hadn't dreamt since living with my grandpaps forty years ago—resurfaces, and I wake up whimpering, drenched in sweat, and lying in a pool of piss. It's the nightmare of what my boyhood mind deemed "The Claw," much like that walking hand from the Addams Family, but with a couple notable exceptions: the Claw is four-fingered, and the Claw is beautifully manicured with long fingernails splashed in bloodred polish. A woman's hand. My mother's hand, quite possibly, although I'm pretty sure my mom had ten fingers from the little I remember about her.

When the Claw scuttles in my dreams, it taps around like a demonic crab. Its clamorous movements echo in the shadowy corridors of my frightened mind. One night, I manage to fall asleep only to wake up with the Claw latched to my face, trying to scratch my eyes out. I scream, only to jerk awake and begin sobbing my fucking brains out, the Claw nowhere to be seen, blood streaming down my cheeks. In the bathroom, I notice hunks of bloodied skin underneath my fingernails. I slap myself across my marred cheeks a few times. The pain is awful and pure comfort.

One day, worse becomes worser when I see a UPS man striding up the street with an envelope in hand. He rings the doorbell and struts away. I scoop the envelope up and go inside, tearing it open to find a stack of paperwork declaring "Adult Emancipation." A sticky note is stuck to the front in Thom's handwriting:

Just do the right thing.

I've had enough. I call Darla, even though she made it clear to never call her under any circumstances. All calls should be directed to her lawyer. Of course she doesn't answer. I call her again intending to leave a voicemail that I believe will be the most epic voicemail ever, where I lay all my thoughts out and give her something real meaty to chew on about how she needs to rethink our marriage, and how good it has been—I have graph papers full of memories to back this up—but instead I leave a half-assed, stuttering, ambiguous message about how I had coffee with Thom, and ordered too many muffins, and he said he's divorcing me.

After a while, with still no response from Darla, I text Darla's sister, Angelica, to see if, perhaps, she could nudge her sister along. She doesn't respond. And neither does Judd, Angelica's husband. Neither does Darla's friend from work, CeCe, who used to hang with Darla. Neither does Jericho, Darla's cousin, who I used to buy weed butter from. I'm about to dial Darla's mom who is suffering from dementia, but I hesitate, my finger trembling in midair. I know that calling Darla's mom is taking it too far.

I dial anyway. It rings.

Darla's mom answers.

"Hello," I say.

Her voice cracks. "Thom, is that you?"

"Uh." I stop. Consider hanging up. But I keep talking. "Yeah. Hey . . . Grandma."

"Thom, so good to hear from you. I want to thank you for that drawing you made of me. You know the one?

Where I'm standing on a grassy field and the sun is beaming overhead. I have the picture taped to the wall over here. I see it every day. And I think of you."

"Thanks, Grandma. I appreciate that. I miss you too."

"You sound so old now. Worn down. Puberty is a real bitch, isn't it?"

She laughs.

I smile. I haven't smiled in a long time. So I keep talking. "You, uh, still collecting thimbles?"

It's the only thing I remember about Darla's mom. All the goddamn thimbles.

"Of course I'm still collecting thimbles. I just got three new ones over the eBay. It's amazing what you can do with that. How sweet of you, by the way! You amaze me so much. You know that. With a father like you had, I'm proud of what you made of yourself. Most boys like you would be dead or strung-out in a gutter by now. No offense, Tommy, but I hope they've locked your father up. I always hated how Darla ended up with that schmuck. That man shouldn't be out in society—"

I hang up. I can't listen anymore. My body thrums with a feverish incandescence. My legs are meshes of electrified wire. I stand up, nearly toppling over, and stumble to the kitchen in the hopes of trying to eat, even a morsel, but once I'm there, my body revolts. I can't stomach the thought of taking one bite. Which is saying something since I'm down to a daily diet of a couple slices of moldy white bread with a thin layer of mayo, the last dregs of what I'm able to scrape from the sides of the jar.

    I opt for a beer instead and lie down in the middle of the sticky kitchen floor, and wait.

viii.
fill in the blanks

Time passes. An hour or two or three, maybe sixteen. Enough time that I can feel my brain congealing into a wad of spat tobacco.

The next morning, I pop one of my few remaining Addies to get me going. I absent-mindedly start cleaning my Mr. Joe coffeemaker with a Q-tip in the stinky fuzzy-gray slippers and flannel robe that I'm pretty sure is Darla's dead father's he left behind when he visited years ago. A light scratchy knock comes at the door, and I nearly scream because it reminds me of the Claw.

I move to the window and peer outside. It's Dmitri, the moving "consultant" from Buttery Bullshit Moving Services. His truck is out front and he's got one of his admirably fake smiles plastered on his lips.

I open the door. "Good morning," Dmitri says, inhaling the air. Chicken Biscuit lurks behind him with a lollipop jutting from his mouth. "I'm sure it's so lovely to begin your day with my friendly voice!"

"Uh-huh. Just like a Rush song," I mutter, throwing up in my mouth a little.

Dimitri then takes one look at my butchered face from the Claw's scratches, and his breath hitches. "Well..." His smile flickers like a bad cable connection. "I come with super news. My men are able to find most of your stuff. We do apologize for the inconveniences. And we would be happy if you leave a five-star review on Yelp..."

I wave Dmitri in, and they go to work unloading boxes and furniture into the house while I resume cleaning Mr. Joe. I ignore their thumps and, at one point, shattering of broken glass, but otherwise, by the time I'm finished with the coffeemaker they are done with the moving.

When I go into the living room, I stop, marveling at what's sitting before me: a plastic-wrapped floral couch, like one of those you'd find in the welcome lobby of a retirement home or a funeral parlor. Definitely not mine. I'm about to raise the issue, when Dmitri and Chicken Biscuit wave goodbye and slip out the door.

I contemplate chasing them down in my stinky slippers, but then grow curious and open a box. The boxes, too, contain items not my own, and apparently are those of an elderly couple named Cherry and Leon McGuire, according to their death certificates found in the *Essentials* box. I also find photos of the couple over the years. Hugging each other on a beach somewhere, their faces wearing tight smiles. Cherry in climbing gear on a cliff. Birthday cakes, and swimming pools, and school photos, and fill in the blanks.

After rummaging through the other boxes, I hang up a display of decorative china dishes adorned with varying kinds of orchids, set out a porcelain candy dish onto an antique coffee table that is remarkably different from my mangled IKEA one, and position picture frames on various side tables of when the couple was younger—family photos with their kids and a golden retriever. I sigh. Darla, Thom, and I never had a golden retriever . . . I don't think.

Once done with the living room, I meander up to the master bedroom and find a bulky, wooden, broken-in bed. I lie down, and the mattress nearly swallows me whole. The mattress has to be older than the bed frame.

As I head to the kitchen, an unfamiliar shadow shifts in my periphery. I turn. My home office door is wide open. Dmitri and his associate must have dropped a few items in there.

I drift over to the doorway, averting my gaze from Elijah Wood, keeping my eyes to the floor. I don't think I can bare to look at him at the moment.

The home office is empty. No boxes. No furniture. Nothing.

I turn to leave the room, and as I do, I peek up at the poster for a millisecond. The poster's afterimage floats in my mind's eye, and something immediately rubs me the wrong way. The afterimage doesn't match what I remember from the original poster. After a momentary hesitation, I turn and take in a real eyeful. My proceeding gasp is fitting for any Oscar-worthy performance (not something Elijah Wood has been acquainted with, I might add).

Elijah Wood is gone. The rest of the poster remains intact—the crimson background and the snow-white words, the cedar trees, a shadowy figure standing in the house. But Elijah Wood's image is nowhere to be found.

And worst of all, his devil fork is missing too.

ix.
garlic babies

"The visceral potency of a dream lessens over your lifetime," Dr. Singh writes in the introduction of his book. "In midlife, you are grappling with this truth."

So, why, Dr. Singh, do my dreams seem to be getting more potent? I wanna ask. That's how it feels, as even in sunlight, I prowl about my house suspicious of my surroundings. Flutters of movement catch my eye, as if the house were infested with rats. I hear wood creaking where there was never any wood. At any moment, I'm expecting to see Elijah Wood's little boyish face peer out of a doorway, ready to pounce and gut me with his two-pronged fork.

I'm pacing in the living room when a flash makes me turn and shriek, and I realize it's a reflection of myself in a window.

"Son of a bitch," I mutter and stumble outside. Maybe fresh air will help, even if the sun's relentless brightness is making me sick. I walk loops around the front yard, then migrate to the backyard, to my garlic garden, which I haven't checked in several weeks.

"Holy shit," I say as I approach it—not only have the green garlic shoots grown in size, but they are gargantuan, taller than me. I take one of the shoots and pull as hard as I can, like I'm playing tug-of-war with the Earth. The shoot slips out of my hands and I fall on my ass. I hurry inside and find a shovel that was among the McGuires' stuff and head back out to the garden where I dig around the shoot until the metal shovel clangs against something hard.

I reach down and extract a garlic bulb, but it's much, much bigger than it should be. The size of a hefty watermelon. I pick it up with two hands, *ohhhhhh*ing at its girth. I can't believe it. Either garlic is a lot bigger than it used to be, or my green thumb is much greener than I could ever imagine . . .

I give the garlic bulb a few gentle pats, shushing it, and place it back into its hole. "Take as much time as you need," I whisper, and proceed to cover it back over with the dirt pile.

Later that afternoon, I am lying on the moldy love seat when I hear a crash upstairs, near the guest bedroom if I have to guess. I roll off to my feet and grab hold of the Viking cleaver knife resting on the coffee table.

I listen for another half hour, and sure enough, more unidentifiable noises rumble throughout the house, like my stomach after eating too many mayo sandwiches. I determine a presence is unsettling the house. Or not just any presence. *Him.* Is he in here now? I wonder. Is he lurking about? Those tapping sounds I hear in between the floors, are they pipes creaking or is it Elijah Wood squirming his way through my house undetected?

At one point, when the furnace cuts on, the home office door slams shut and I tense up, imagining a scenario where Elijah Wood lunges at me with his devil fork and I punch him square between his Earth-shaped eyeballs. Not something I want to do. But none of this I want. Not a new life as a superhero Mid-Lifer. Not a new house to call my own, or at least not a house half crowded with items owned by a dead couple named the McGuires. And certainly I never, ever wanted Elijah Wood in my home—but what is there to do?

This is where I am.

I open Dr. Singh's book to distract myself and continue reading: "The future is the Mid-Lifer's cape. Don your cape now. See the past falling back behind you like tumbling dominos. Up ahead rests a glorious, stubbornly bright light of any color you want that light to be. And how you get to that light is your superpower. Is it a new car? A new hobby? A new adventure? A new religion? A new companion? Take the time to really ask yourself: What will be my one superpower?"

I reread this passage multiple times, too distracted to understand the words, nursing the Viking knife. I try to think what a little goblin like Elijah Wood would do. Where would he hide? And when do Elijah Woods make themselves known? At night, under a full moon? Or when I'm sitting down for my morning coffee? I take out my phone and google *How to trap an Elijah Wood* but nothing worthwhile pops up.

Then an idea comes to me. Maybe watching the movie once and for all will answer some of these questions.

With much reluctance, I turn the movie on, this time vowing to myself that I will get to the end of it, at whatever cost. The movie is just about to begin when my phone starts ringing. It's Darla. As it rings, I take a deep breath and relax my shoulders. Should my voice sound mad, happy, bored? I tap the screen with a shaky finger to answer.

"Hey," I say. I sound bored.

"I don't have much time to talk, so I will come out with it. I'm about to move to California."

"Wait, what? When are you moving to California?"

"In like fifteen minutes."

"What . . . Why are you . . . ?"

"I need a change of scenery, and LA is calling my name. Plus, I need to be closer to my mom. Anyway, the moving truck is about to leave now. Dmitri might bring over one more box for you at some point in the future, some Polaroids of Thom and other random memorabilia."

"Okay."

There's a brief silence and in that silence, I can picture Darla's expression. I know she is trying not to cry because I hear her swallowing multiple times.

"FUUUUUUCK!" she howls.

"Uh, are you okay?"

"What do you think?"

"Guess not," I say.

"It's just . . . like . . . that's all you got? After all these years, after all the shit we've been through together, all you got is . . . *'Okay*'?"

"Sorry. I don't know what to say."

"Jesus, man . . . Well, I was going to text you this, but I guess I will just come out and say it now, as uneasy as that is."

She clears her throat, and I hear her take a suck of her pinky.

"Our marriage . . . it was real to me, a long time ago. I fucking loved you, and I would like to believe you loved me too. But somehow, somewhere, at some time, I don't know how or even when . . . it ended, unbeknownst to me. Maybe unbeknownst to either of us. And now here we are, standing too far away from each other to hear what the other is saying . . . Which I can finally see now that the only thing that held us together all this time was . . . Thom." She pauses, sucks a little more. "Which means, without Thom, we are two strangers living together. I don't want to live with a stranger . . . do you?"

"I don't know."

"I don't think you do . . ." She stops, blows her nose. "I can't do this anymore. It seems pointless to talk about because I'm moving to California in, now, ten minutes. I'm sorry to end it like this, I'm really sorry. But you also didn't fight for it. You were too strung-out half the time to care." Another silence follows, and I think she's hung up, but then she speaks again. "It might be true that our marriage went to a shit-basket, but we made Thom together. And for that reason, I will always be grateful I met you at that Necrophiliac Hamsters show."

I cut in and inform her it wasn't a Necrophiliac Hamsters show, but a Robot Cocks one.

"It wasn't," she insists. "I know it wasn't. I *love* Hamsters. I *hate* Robot Cocks. I would have never gone to IHOP with you if it had been a Robot Cocks show. I would have been too pissy."

I cut in and inform her we went to a Waffle House, not IHOP.

"This is what I'm talking about," she says with a Thom-sigh. "The point is, maybe one day we will see each other again. And maybe when that happens we'll be completely different people. Maybe not. But for now . . . it's over, I guess. Just . . . I wish you would . . . take care, okay? I gotta go . . . bye . . ."

I hear sadness in her voice, then she hangs up, and I remain affixed to my position on the love seat, staring out a side window at a leaf-less tree, for what must be hours. Only then do my parting words for Darla formulate.

I want to say that I own a quaint little broken-down house on Crooked Way, with its own home office, a beautiful view of a forest, and a garden of garlic growing bountifully. I want to tell her that I'm nearly finished with Dr. Singh's introduction about how to be a better person during a midlife crisis, and that I plan to do yoga regularly, and eat leafier greens, and recycle my beer cans, and meditate every morning, and start a woodworking hobby, and buy a new outfit that doesn't consist of hole-ridden T-shirts of deceased punk bands from my youth.

I want to tell her that when I get to the other side of this, whatever *this* may be, yes, I might very well be a completely different person.

X.
a cornucopia of corpse colors

The next morning, after speaking to Darla for maybe the last time, I encounter something unimaginably horrible lying in the middle of the kitchen floor. And worst of all, I step on it before I see it. The sound it makes is what I imagine the sound to be if someone were to pluck one of my eyeballs out and bite down on it like a maraschino cherry.

A juicy splat.

I look down to a rotting, decaying avocado. Only after I have cleaned what looks like dogshit off the bottom of my foot, and popped a couple uppers, and drank a salad bowl of coffee, do I ask the question that needs to be asked.

How the hell did this avocado get in my house?

Dr. Singh's imagined voice swirls in my head: "Fearing an aspect of your past is not dissimilar to letting a measly splinter poison your blood to your death. Have the superhero courage to dig out that splinter now!"

That old vinyl record that Grandpaps used to mention begins spinning in my head.

Is it possible Thom put the avocado in here? That he snuck in here last night, set the avocado on the floor, and left? Or maybe Darla did it as she was headed to the airport for her move to California? Or maybe Darla had her lawyer do it? Or maybe it was Dmitri? Or Chicken Biscuit? Or maybe it was none of them and somehow along the way I placed it there?

No fucking way.

I inspect the kitchen, including all the cabinets, opening them, examining the dirty, mouse-dropping-infested shelves within them, believing I might stumble upon some smoking-gun clue. But there's nothing of the sort. Unless the avocado rolled into my house on its own volition—very unlikely.

I ponder the empty cabinets for a while, probably hours, as evidenced by the sunrays elongating across my body, turning my face into a sundial. I don't know what to do about this situation. I don't know if I even believe it. But speculation becomes murkier when I hear an audible, disappointed sigh behind me—a Thom sigh—and lurch around to find nothing except what I can only describe as stale, uncirculated air.

"Thom?" I call. The house only responds with a creak in the distance and a drip drip drip of water from a leaky pipe.

I go outside while there's still daylight and take a stroll to my garlic babies, only to see that there's a hole dug in the ground. In a panic, I rush over and confirm that one of my giant garlic babies has been excavated from the earth.

"Son of a motherfucking bitch," I croak.

When I get inside, I scoop up the Viking knife and stalk around the house, going from room to room.

"Where you at, little motherfucker?" I say, not sure why I feel the need to call someone, even someone like a demonic B-list actor, a "little motherfucker"—seems superfluous—but those are the words that have been injected into my tongue.

"Come out, little motherfucker," I say as I move upstairs to the guest room that could have, should have, been, Thom's, but is now filled with the McGuires' junk. Then my master bedroom. But again I find squat. Not even a crumb of evidence that Elijah Wood has been creeping about. Still only that squashed avocado from the kitchen.

I leave the home office for last. When I'm back downstairs, I watch its door from down the hall, waiting for a reasonable plan to percolate. A small strip of light from the setting sun creates a glow underneath the door. The light flickers, and I hear what I assume to be the shuffling of feet.

"You in there, little motherfucker?" I call. My voice sounds like crushed gravel, mainly from lack of use and dehydration but also from the fact that I'm shaking to the core. My body feels dipped in menthol. I'm scared out of my rational wits. Worse than watching those horror movies with Thom. I'm seeing now that it's different when you're living in a horror movie.

I back away and hide in the broom closet, waiting.

Night comes. I drift upstairs, letting the McGuires' bed engulf me. Drowsy. Withdrawing from the various pills I took throughout the day. Exhausted from all the pacing and threshing and twitching. Sleep comes too quickly for somebody whose whole body is experiencing what a lightning rod must feel. My eyes seal shut like two dusty tombs.

And then they snap open, and I wake up to a face hovering above me, through the hole where a ceiling fan used to be. It's too dark for me to discern details, but the face stares back at me, wide-eyed, focused, brimming with too much curiosity, like I'm some kind of dismembered insect in a glass display case. My senses come to life. It's him. Elijah Wood. I blink a few times, and the face vanishes, followed by the tapping of wood as he scurries off.

I get out of bed and, first, go to lock the door, only to remember that the door doesn't have a knob, so I scoot one of the McGuires' huge-ass armoires over, nearly giving myself a hernia in the process. I retrieve the Viking knife from underneath my pillow and pace the room, inspecting for any entry points besides the ceiling hole.

As I get to one corner of the room, wood cracks, and my foot goes straight through the floor. The wooden floorboard splinters and penetrates my foot. I cry out fiercely, dropping the knife somewhere. The cuts are deep in my foot, and for some reason, the pain is interwoven with giddiness, like taking a nice, prolonged hit of nitrous oxide.

Then I remember why I came over here to begin with. Elijah Wood. I snatch a piece of floorboard leaning against the wall that the previous owners never repaired and use it as a weapon. Unknown to me, though, the floorboard is lined with thick nails. One of the nails goes deep into my hand, and this time I rattle off a scream that reverberates through the walls—like the opening to that All That Remains song where the lead singer unleashes a hellaciously charged metalcore growl that could shift the tectonic plates. I toss the floorboard aside, rubbing my hands on the floor to find the knife in the darkness.

A voice, coming from somewhere nearby. Overhead? Underneath? From where the floorboard cracked open? From the door? Hell if I know. My hearing is shot, gone, sand-dusted down by all those hours I'd spent destroying them with cramped concert venues. All I know is the voice is whispery and fizzy.

Do it again, the voice says.

"What the fuck you say to me?" I garble.

Do it again.

"Thom . . . is that you?"

Show me what you can do, Daddy.

I mentally chew on this, because the voice most certainly resembles Thom's. Maybe only as much as a donkey resembles a stallion, but still. Despite it being a poser voice, an imitation—as if Thom's voice were droplets of blood in a hypodermic needle—it makes me think of Thom.

"Thom, that you?" I call up, spotting the Viking knife near the bed and picking it up.

One more time, Daddy. Please.

"Okay . . . But . . ." I sputter, then swallow, thinking about what is being implied here. What *Thom* is implying, what *Thom's voice* is implying. As I mull, the pain of my wounds starts to tingle my senses.

I stumble back over to the floorboard of nails and stare at it.

Yesssssss, Daddy.

The voice's hiss tickles the back of my neck. I jerk around, peering up at the hole in the ceiling. A ghost of movement. A shadowy imprint of a devil's fork. I brandish the Viking knife higher. But the harder I stare, the more there's nothing but a black hole. Same with the hole in the floor. Darkness is crowding me. Another Thom-sigh from somewhere. A silvery glint of steel flashes from the corner of the room.

"Come out, little motherfucker," I growl.

The record in my head spins faster and faster, vortexing. I swear I hear music seeping through that giant crack in the house's foundation. Songs of jaw-breaking and teeth-gnashing bloodsport, their crashing melodies scrubbing my brain like steel wool. The intro to The Clash's "Know Your Rights" is in there. So is the chorus to Pennywise's "Wouldn't It Be Nice." The bridge to NOFX's "Linoleum." The outro to Heavens to Betsy's "Nothing Can Stop Me."

A warlock's whirling pot of punk.

The distortion sings through my veins.

BA-BUM-BA-DA-DUM-DUM

BUM-BA-BUM-BA-BUM-BAM

DUMMMM-DUMMMM

BABABABABABABABABBA

Amidst the distortion, the Thom voice continues to speak.

Skewer me with your pain, Daddy.

"IS THAT WHAT YOU WANT!?" I scream back, trying to dagger through the music, but my voice dies off into the noise.

I drop the Viking knife and overturn the piece of floorboard so the moon-tipped nails now point heavenward.

I take a step.

Stop.

A Thom memory suddenly whips into my mind.

When Thom was five or six and we went shore fishing on Lake Hartwell. I got so drunk that I wandered off and passed out in a bush, only to wake up to Thom screaming frantically, covered in mud.

"No, no," I groan.

More arsenic-laced memories such as these, the ones buried deeper than any garlic babies could go, spring to the surface left and right, and suddenly the moonlit-tipped nails are calling my name, inviting me over.

There you go, Daddy, the voice eggs me on. I take another step forward. Yup, that's Thom's voice . . . if it were kneaded down by the gnarled hands of a depraved war criminal. Grandpaps's hands.

"There I go *what?*" I say, wiping the sweat from my face with my bloodied hand.

No response.

"There I go fucking what?" I belt out, my voice dissolving into a gurgle.

I stomp out a rhythm with my foot, the bloodied one. The music enveloping the house pounds with it.

"*Thom!* You in my house or what, dude? Speak to me, godfuckingdammit. SPEAKTOME!"

Another memory flashes. Thom and I playing hide-and-seek when Darla was out of town, and me taking fuck-knows-what and falling asleep in my hiding spot, waking up five hours later to pounding at the front door and opening it to find a disgruntled neighbor and a blubbery Thom.

The darkness pushes farther inward. Shadows blacken. The corners of the room are not far from what the corners of my mind are—empty spaces where the devil likes to hide.

"Tellmewhatyouneed—"

Please, Daddy, finish what you sssssstarted.

The voice has changed. It's grizzlier, re-formed into stainless steel. Grandpaps's voice?

The music swells, and with it comes another memory.

When Thom was thirteen or fourteen, and I was given the task of picking him and a few friends up from the movies when Darla got stuck at work. I was already too stoned and buzzed to be driving, maybe even a little drunk, because as I pulled up and Thom was getting into the car with his friends, I *accidentally*—that's the word I used to explain it to Darla—puked all over my lap.

Keep going.

"Stop it, no," I whimper.

Keep going—or else.

"I don't want to. Please don't make me . . ."

What did I just say?

The voice slices into me, making me cower.

OR ELSE.

Don't disobey me.

"Please, Daddy—"

Now, the voice yowls, and my knees nearly buckle at the venom-infused tone.

You want this to be over with, don't you?

I nod.

Then take your fucking punishment.

I nod again, take a step, the nails sinking into the flesh of my bare foot. Tears instantly stream down my cheeks, intermixing with the blood.

That's it. That's the way.

The piece of floorboard is now stuck to my foot. I fall down on my ass, ripping it away, opening the wound further. Despite the darkness, I can picture a heavy river of blood spewing forth. The pain is so much, so blindingly white-hot, that I begin cackling like a deranged hyena, collapsing into a fetal position and squeezing my eyes shut, a blaze of stars alighting on the backs of my eyelids.

"How's . . . th-that, Daddy?" I spit out, drool dripping from my chin.

No response.

"Was that good enough?"

Still no response.

"I said, *HOWSTHAT?*"

The music from faraway cuts off abruptly.

I open my eyes.

I've been cast in total darkness. The moonlight leaking into the window has vanished, blocked by something. Stale, uncirculated air. Then the presence shifts.

From somewhere up ahead, I hear scuttling, like a mouse running away.

Or was that the Claw?

Or was it Thom or Elijah Wood or maybe Grandpaps, who never cut his toenails?

"Who's there?" I breathe, my voice hoarse.

I listen some more, but there's only silence. Not the comforting kind. It's the silence one hears when their coffin is shut for good. Vacuous. Those two or three seconds in between songs, dragging interminably on. A silence that requires filling.

I pound the floor hard with my hand, the undamaged one, until my knuckles are mutilated. Then I curl up on the floor near the foot of the bed and close my eyes again, summoning a drone of noise in my imagination. A disturbed hornet's nest. A chain saw whirring to life. A blade striking my grandpaps's whetstone. A Robot Cocks show with Darla.

This last image takes hold, and eventually lulls me to sleep.

When I wake up, daylight is pouring through the dirty panes of the window. My hand, scabbed over with dried blood, has already started to spiderweb with yellow-tinged infection, and my feet are swollen ten times their normal size, starting to darken yellow and red and blue—a cornucopia of corpse colors. It won't be long, I think, before they explode like one of those avocados, and all the decaying meat will squirt out in a fireworks display of liquefied flesh, splashing my eyes and cheeks and hair.

Sometime later in the morning, I scoot across the room, get up, and, with considerable pain, move the heavy-ass armoire from the door, all the while thinking that I need a plan, or things might get worse.

xi.
come to daddy

By evening, my wounds are like breathtaking fields of multicolored poppies. They pulsate with the beating of my heart. I know I should call somebody for help, but then it hits me. Who am I going to call? Thom, who has divorced me? Darla, who has also divorced me? Darla's lawyer, who doesn't answer my calls? Maybe Darla's mom, who has dementia and thinks I'm Thom? An ambulance, which will cost me upward of thirty grand? Any options boil down to one option—waiting and seeing how this whole situation plays out. At the very least, I'm lucky enough to have found some expired pain pills in one of the dead McGuires' boxes.

As nighttime arrives, I execute a plan, knowing that Elijah Wood will be coming back out of his mysterious hiding spot. This time, I will be ready to capture him once and for all, even if I'm two sneezes away from being a bona fide invalid.

I belly-crawl into the broom closet and wait, listening for footsteps, picturing what a fight would look like between a Viking cleaver knife and a two-pronged devil's fork. One hard chop from a cleaver knife will inflict far more damage than a fork stab, right? Given my state, the key will be to stab him in the leg and when he goes down, hold the knife against his throat and demand he give me some answers, tell me where my garlic baby has disappeared to.

It's the middle of the night when I hear a knock at the front door. I raise myself to my knees, holding the knife up high. I wait. A knock comes again. And then again.

I manage to get to my feet and slink from my hiding spot, maneuvering about the dark house like a sepsis-ridden faerie sprite. I peer out the window to the front porch, and a figure waits on the doorstep.

"Yeah?" I yell.

"It's me, Daddy." It's Thom's voice. Or sounds like it.

I cut on the living room light and crack the front door a tinge. Peering out, I cannot make out a face, but the eyes—holy shit, those eyes could land a jet in a rainstorm.

It's Elijah Wood. Or at least the appearance of a man who could be Elijah Wood.

"Who is it?" I ask, as if the answer isn't already on display in front of me.

"Let me in, Daddy."

I don't say anything because what am I supposed to say? All I can think about is where the hell is he hiding that devil fork?

"I brought stuff for dinner," he says. "And a bottle of wine, although I know you hate wine, so I brought you Pepsi. In glass bottles, like you had as a kid."

I'm so gobsmacked that I proceed to mindlessly open the door the whole way and examine him under the light more closely. Yeah, it's confirmed, it's Elijah Wood, at least on the surface. He's as short as I expected him to be. More than five feet, but barely so. In one hand, he's holding a paper grocery bag with a baguette sticking out, and in the other hand, a plate of roughly chopped garlic cloves wrapped in plastic. No devil fork that I can see.

"Can I come in?" he asks again, smirking.

Again, no words come out of my mouth. I stand back slightly, a gesture of an invitation. He enters into the living room and does a 360 survey of the house.

"Not bad, Daddy. I wasn't sure you could make it work, but you have," he says, and these words strike like a power chord because, well, these are exactly the words Thom would say if he ever came to visit—before, you know, he divorced me. He would do just as Elijah has done and do a 360 survey and say, *Not bad, Dad.*

When Elijah turns back to me, I scrutinize his face. Beneath those vivid, piercing eyes, there's something alive, like looking into a sun-drenched well and seeing a snake writhing at the bottom. A vibrancy exists deep in his irises that signal to me that Thom is living in there. Thom's gaze is staring back at me, as if he'd stumbled upon an uber-realistic Halloween mask of Elijah Wood and donned it.

"Daddy?" Elijah says. "Did you hear me?"

"What?"

"Why are you holding . . . ?" He points with his head to the Viking knife in my hand.

"I don't know," I say, as I look him up and down, searching.

"Ahh, the fork." He pulls up his pant leg to reveal the fork holstered to his leg. He slides it out, and I take a step back. "Don't worry. It's decorative. See?" He stabs his stomach with it. Nothing happens. It's a prop.

"By the way, I had to dig up one of your garlic bulbs. I hope that's okay, because I'm going to make the best damn garlic bread you've ever tasted. With pasta, of course."

"Okay."

"I'll go ahead and start on it. Where's the kitchen?"

I point to a door to the right, and Elijah smiles warmly, except again it's the way Thom smiles, the way he tugs his lips up ever so slightly. Not a full cheek-to-cheek smile, but one of those playful smirks that wrinkles the chin.

My jaw dangles open as I watch Elijah disappear into the kitchen.

Some minutes later, I follow him in there.

xii.
glimpsing the other side way ahead

The smell of the garlic is intoxicating. I'm sipping on a glass bottle of Pepsi while Thom, who continues to wear his Elijah Wood mask, flies around the kitchen with dexterity, somehow already knowing where to find the things he needs. He hums a Poison song as he works, definitely a Thom-like thing to do while he's cooking. *Nothing makes me cook better than hair bands,* Thom once said—or maybe that was Darla who said that?

A timer goes off, and Thom jauntily comes over with a steaming plate of angel hair pasta topped with red sauce. He places it on the table in front of me, along with a sizable hunk of yellowy garlic bread.

"The angel didn't scream too loudly in the making of this pasta," Thom says, sitting down at the table with his own plate.

I look over and he's got a deadpan expression. Just like Thom—to crack a backwards-ass joke about murdering an angel without even so much as a grin.

"I'm glad we could do this, finally, you know," he says, taking the first bite.

I nod.

We both eat in silence. The pasta is splendid, buttery and garlicky, al dente with a spicy red sauce that makes my mouth tingle. The bread is even better. Crunchy, with a perfect blend of fresh garlic and butter, topped with sage and parsley.

After we finish eating, we sip on some wine from chipped mugs. I hate wine as much as I hate the Bee Gees, but, in observance of this scrumptious meal, I swallow it back to show my thanks to Thom—whose Elijah Wood eyes bear down on me.

"How many pasta dinners do you think we've had over the years?" he asks.

"Well . . . too many," I respond, licking the remaining sauce from my fork.

"It makes me think about what if memories were things we could sort through. Wouldn't that be cool? If we could throw certain ones away, and keep others close by."

"Like your rock—"

"—collection," Thom finishes my sentence, and we both laugh at the same time because if there is one thing I did right as a daddy, it was to help my son build the biggest rock collection this side of the Mississippi. Sometimes, when I encountered a gravel lot during a walk, I came home with my pockets stuffed full of rocks.

"This can't be it, can it?" Thom says.

"What?"

"Our last meal together."

Thom's eyes flicker then, as if his Elijah Wood mask were becoming less a mask and more his actual face. To my dismay, he's losing his Thom-ness.

"I gotta go back to where I came from," he says.

"Not yet," I assert. My jaw bounces up and down, the words brewing right on my tongue like the scalding coffee from Brü's, and then I begin to speak, eloquently and fluidly. That the first time I held him, it felt like I was holding a hunk of radiant stardust. I go on to tell him that my love for him feels like what I feel when I see a fast-moving river with wild water rapids. Or that my love for him is like when one of my favorite bands plays my favorite song, and I can just let it loose from my lips and scream it out from the lungs, and there are hundreds of other people around me screaming it out, too, and the crowd becomes one, connected by the loud, chaotic kismet of the sound. I tell him that I have wronged him terribly, and that I will live with those splinters of regret until the day I die—whether that's sooner or later. He never deserved a daddy like me, but I also didn't deserve my own daddy, and so can we please, in the near or distant future, meet in the middle once again?

He accepts my words with a nod, and even stands up and comes around the table and gives me a side hug, which makes me wince, but I take the pain, because I feel I deserve every second of it.

"Where are you going from here?" I ask him as he sits back down across from me.

"It's not about where I'm going. It's about . . . I've got a feel for this place, and now that I have my feel, I move on to the next one."

"Alright, then."

"You could say I am passing through, a visitor or a guest, whatever you prefer, but it's not the length of time that matters. It's that it happened at all. And I'm damn grateful for the time. You were a good daddy. I just want you to know that."

My eyes start to prickle. Moisture crests at the corners. Actual tears? It's been so long, I can hardly recall the sensation.

"But, you know," he continues, "I think you deserved a last meal, cooked by your one and only—a parting gift, as insignificant as it may seem. Because, well . . ."

The tears push through and stream down my cheeks.

"I love you."

He waits for me to swallow my phlegm. "I love you too . . ."

Elijah—it's definitely Elijah Wood again—is then standing up to leave, and I'm standing up with him, despite my body throbbing all over. He gives me a tight, excruciating hug and for just a moment I feel two sharp points at the base of my neck. Not sharp enough as to pierce the skin but sharp enough that I wonder if there's a fork pressing into me, or maybe the talons of a claw?

He withdraws from our embrace, and I see the last remnants of Thom have faded away.

"Don't take him," I blurt out, and he turns, facing me again. "Don't take him with you." More tears come pouring down my cheeks. "Please."

Amusement crinkles his eyes, and briefly, I see what Elijah sees. Me. A broken-down, pathetic, middle-aged nobody, with no friends, no family, juiced for all I'm worth. In his vision, I'm not far off from what I see when I look down at a squashed avocado after stepping on it. Bruised, rotten, decaying fruit.

"That's not how it works. You know that," he says.

"Just . . . just . . . stay awhile. A little longer, can't you? Let me make some coffee . . . *Anything* . . . Don't make me get on my knees."

He looks down at my hand and the Viking knife shaking in it.

"I will see you later, Daddy," is all he says, then he slinks down the hallway into the darkness of the home office. I wait and listen for confirmation that he's gone, a door closing or a thump or the chime of a bell. I don't know what I'm expecting, but there's only thick silence.

After a while, I hobble after him and see the office door standing wide open. I lean against the doorway and flick on the overhead light that buzzes to life. Elijah is back where he's supposed to be.

I stare at the poster again and realize I don't feel that same itching anxiety as I did before. I no longer see Elijah and think of atrophy, and destruction, and chaos. Instead, I picture Thom, walking aimlessly from one place to another, until he finds himself strolling over a bridge and glimpsing the other side way ahead of him.

With one foot in front of the other, I'm confident he will be home soon enough.

[hidden track]

"See the future as not two diverging paths but as you holding a scythe, able to chop away the brush if they obscure your way. Only you can forge your own path into the Midlife."

This is how the introduction to Dr. Singh's book ends. And so that's what I'm going to do. I'm going to spend my time cutting down a path with my Viking knives, my last days in my home, imagining it as an album I dub *When Life Is Falling to Shit All Around You*. The music will be cranked to the highest it can go. MxPx and Bad Religion, into the ska punk of Squad 5-O and Voodoo Glow Skulls and the Chipmonks, leaning harder into the Bruisers and the Robot Cocks and the Shitlickers, into the realms of rage-encumbered grindcore like the Dillinger Escape Plan and the Tony Danza Tapdance Extravaganza Band. Their wall of unforgiving decibels will deafen me even more than I've already been deafened from hearing them over the years.

I also imagine finding myself finally sitting down and watching *Come to Daddy* to the very end, and discovering why Elijah Wood is so scared and desperate on that movie poster. I learn why his two-pronged fork holds significance, and why the daddy shadow floating in the poster's background is just that—a shadow. I imagine getting to the end of the movie, and suddenly an epiphany descending upon me. All the recent months will make sense—all the divorces and oversized garlic bulbs and graph paper. I picture the floorboards underneath my feet beginning to warp even more, snapping even more loudly, the ever-ballooning ceiling in the living room giving out and bursting forth with all of the second floor's contents gushing down on a tidal wave of useless crap, furniture and decorative fixtures and lamps and framed pictures and outdated bed frames owned by dead people crushing me underneath their weight, burying me like a worm deep beneath the soil.

I would like to believe that I will eventually wiggle myself out, and retreat to the yard, and nestle into the dirt next to my garlic babies and continue to squirm about, as I witness my final show. The house imploding. The very last song. The swan song. The song after the encore song, when the whole crowd is so jacked up on drugs and booze and adrenaline and spunk and unadulterated youth that they demand the band douse them with one final ear-bleeding salutation.

I am certain that this swan song before me will be better than any double-bass drums and guitar effects and crashing cymbals and screeching vocals that any band has created. Its cacophony will mash me into a sticky paste, soften me like wet modeling clay, pound me into a piece of sheet metal, like all great punk music was intended to do. Until that old vinyl record in my head tornados itself around so violently that my brain matter, and all my guts to go along with it, will splatter the world.

And when this last song fades away, maybe, just maybe, I will gather myself up again, like I've done before countless times, and keep going on.

Or maybe I won't.

ABOUT THE AUTHORS

DAVID CORSE (he/him) is the pen name for David Cross, a dark fantasy author and movie podcaster from the Midwest. "Mother is Coming Home" is his long-form fiction debut. His untitled dystopian horror novella is coming out in 2025. When not writing, David co-hosts Award Wieners, a pun-filled podcast about Academy Award Best Picture winners. He is also a frequent guest on the Movie, Films & Flix podcast, where he chats about slashers, creature features, and ghosts. You can chat with him on Twitter @itsmedavidcross.

RYAN T. JENKINS (he/him) is based in Williamsburg, Virginia, where he lives with his partner and daughter. With a master's degree in English from Appalachian State University and previously a managing editor for Tor Books, he now runs his own freelancing business and is a contractor for Nightfire, Tor's horror imprint, copyediting and proofreading novels. In addition to freelancing, Ryan T. is an avid reader and writer of horror. His short stories have been published in the anthology *We're Infested!: Tales of Vermin, Insects, and Filth* (edited by Alex Gonzalez), *Hearth & Coffin*, *Twelve Winters*, *Dark Horses*, and *Abandon Journal*. Learn more about his writing at ryantjenkins.com.

ACKNOWLEDGMENTS

DAVID CORSE - This story wouldn't exist without the love and support of my wife, Sarah Klenakis. Thank you for the countless days and nights you spent listening to me talk about the strange people in my head. Thank you for picking me up, holding me, and telling me this story—and my art—was worth pursuing. When I didn't believe in myself, I believed in you instead. I can't wait for the day when it's my turn to lift you up and show the world what a brilliant writer you are.

Thank you also to Alex Ebenstein, Split Scream's editor and champion, for plucking "Mother" from the slush pile and giving it a home. You make everything you touch roar like a T-Rex.

To Alex Woodroe for her kindness, wisdom, and integrity. You encouraged me to lean into my weirdness and use all my senses to tell a story. "Mother" is ooey and gooey because of you.

To my writing pals, Michael Betts, Lauren Bolger, Lauren Coffin, Sam Melville, Steven Patchett, and Michael Pritt. Your invaluable feedback not only made "Mother" a better story but me a better writer. Thank you for adopting a stray like me.

Thanks to Matt Blairstone, Tenebrous Press' founder and publisher, for keeping it real... real Weird. You've built something special, and I'm honored to have a tiny part in it.

To my parents, Don and Sheila Cross, for supporting my dream to be a writer. It took some time, but we did it. I miss you, Dad. This book is for you.

To my brother, Daniel Cross, for watching horror movies with me when we were way too young.

Thanks to Lin Rice, my first beta reader, who read all my terrible stories while I learned how to write fiction.

Blurbing is an act of generosity. Thanks a ton to Mathilda Zeller for giving me her time.

Laurel Hightower, author of "Below," was the first person I met in the horror community, and made me feel at home. You're the best!

To Richard Hauge, my high school creative writing teacher, for instilling a life-long love of writing into an impressionable teen.

I'd also like to thank Lisa Robel née Mueller, my oldest friend, for letting me name the doctor in this story after her. When I came up with the doctor character, I wanted to model her after someone who was compassionate and whip-smart. That's you to a T.

Thanks to the Breakfast Burrito Boys and Girls, my life-long friends and confidants, for always being there. You're all terrible at fantasy football but great at being a friend.

My final thank-you goes to you, the reader, for supporting an independent press. Without you, there'd be less space for authors like me in the world. Every book you purchase from an indie is a vote for more new voices, more diversity, and more genre-pushing horror—HELL YEAH!

RYAN T. JENKINS - This novelette being my first semi-full-length publication, I'm resisting the desire to thank everyone I ever knew, including my fifty-plus first cousins and all my favorite teachers through the years (Dr. Childers, Mrs. Nodine, Dr. Beckley). Whoops okay, I need to stop now. Oh and Ms. Swanson, my high school English teacher—who set my writing path ablaze. Okay, that's it. Now into adult life.

Actually, one more thing. All the bands mentioned—the real ones—were a major part of my youth. As a confused weird-ass kid who couldn't make sense of my extreme introversion, this loud music became an outlet for whatever reason. In fact, the Chipmonks, a band referenced in the hidden track chapter, was a band I played in myself. We were punk, I guess—or pop punk? Or something? Anyway, I had fun playing music with buddies over my teenage years, including Micah, Mike J., Jamin, Drew, Adam, Bobby, and others. Later, I attended shows with Anna and Carl. Okay, now into adulthood, for real this time.

Thanks, first and foremost, to the Muckheads. Natalie, Kristen, Harrison, and John—the true fab four. This story would not exist without this writing group. Thanks very much for y'all's input and wisdom—you made this story live and then soar!

Muchas gracias to the one and only Marco Katz Montiel. Brilliant writer (marcokatz.com), brilliant accountability partner, brilliant friend and person. Thanks, Marco, for your feedback on this story and all the other stories, but most important thanks for standing alongside me as I honed my craft. Whenever I hear an aspiring writer ask, "How do I become a writer?", I think: *Find yourself a Marco Katz*.

Thank you to Nathan Isaksson, who provided invaluable advice and notes on the story. Can't wait to have a table with you at a convention soon!

Thank you to T Van Santana, for their early feedback on this story and their conversations about writing and other illuminating shit.

Thank you to Gordon B. White, who also provided some damn good feedback on this story—i.e., inspired an entire chapter—and ushered me into the writers' realm with perfection.

Thank you to Alex Gonzalez, another face on my personal Mt. Rushmore of artists who made my writing into something real and readable.

To the next Alex—Alex Ebenstein—wow, how did I get so lucky as having you as my first editor? You made this story from a soapbox car into a Maserati. Incredible work. I will respect editors for the rest of my life because of you.

Thanks to everyone at Tenebrous Press, too—Alex Woodroe and Matt Blairstone, whose vision about writing makes me feel like I've found a home. Also, I'm honored to share this volume with David Corse and his masterpiece of a story. I love how our stories play off each other.

Thanks and love to my fam—Mom, Dad, and Carrie. You tolerate my weirdness and aloofness with grace. I'm happy to tell others that this novelette is NOT autobiographical.

Finally, thank you, Evie—you are seven now. Wow. You inspire me every day. In part, this story was written to live every moment reminding myself of how lucky I am to be with you. You are a beautiful and kind person. It's important to note, too, that you cannot use any material in this story for your therapy sessions later in life. The daddy in this story is not your daddy . . . to a certain extent. Love you!

And I love you, genius wife and snake charmer, Ali, who not only gave a wonderful response to this story and has encouraged me along my writing journey, but also provides a gift that no other person gets— VIP access to your brilliant mind with our nightly conversations. I'm out of touch with movies and TV shows now because of you, and I'm okay with that. Thank you for your presence and your lust for life. You are one of a kind. (Now, let's see what you write in your acknowledgments about me. No pressure.)

ABOUT THE ARTISTS

Viviana is a Portuguese artist most known as **ECHO ECHO**. Her creative influence is born in observing nature to the smallest details and recreating that feeling in her illustrations. She likes to create new worlds, bringing some sort of reality to these fantasy worlds while filling them with psychedelic manifestations of her imagination. Find more of her work on Instagram @echoechoillustrations.

EVANGELINE GALLAGHER is an award-winning illustrator from Baltimore, Maryland. They received their BFA in Illustration from the Maryland Institute College of Art in 2018. When they aren't drawing they're probably hanging out with their dog, Charlie, or losing at a board game. They possess the speed and enthusiasm of 10,000 illustrators.

CONTENT WARNINGS

These stories are works of horror fiction which contain dark content that may be triggering to some individuals. In addition to instances and implications of violence and death throughout, both works deal with addiction, and there are instances of elder abuse, implied self-harm, and implied eating disorder in "Mother is Coming Home." Please read with caution.

Grab another Tenebrous title!

Grab another Tenebrous title!

TENEBROUS PRESS

aims to drag the malleable Horror genre into newer, Weirder territory with stories that are incisive, provocative, intelligent and terrifying; delivered by voices diverse and unsung.

FIND OUT MORE:
www.tenebrouspress.com
Social Media @TenebrousPress

NEW WEIRD HORROR

www.ingramcontent.com/pod-product-compliance
Lightning Source LLC
LaVergne TN
LVHW040055080526
838202LV00045B/3651